Torn Lace
and Other Stories

Texts and Translations

Chair: Robert J. Rodini

Series editors: Eugene C. Eoyang, Michael R. Katz, Judith L. Ryan, English Showalter, Mario J. Valdés, and Renée Waldinger

Texts

1. Isabelle de Charrière. *Lettres de Mistriss Henley publiées par son amie.* Ed. Joan Hinde Stewart and Philip Stewart. 1993.
2. Françoise de Graffigny. *Lettres d'une Péruvienne.* Introd. Joan DeJean and Nancy K. Miller. 1993.
3. Claire de Duras. *Ourika.* Ed. Joan DeJean. Introd. Joan DeJean and Margaret Waller. 1994.
4. Eleonore Thon. *Adelheit von Rastenberg.* Ed. and introd. Karin A. Wurst. 1996.
5. Emilia Pardo Bazán. *"El encaje roto" y otros cuentos.* Ed. and introd. Joyce Tolliver. 1996.

Translations

1. Isabelle de Charrière. *Letters of Mistress Henley Published by Her Friend.* Trans. Philip Stewart and Jean Vaché. 1993.
2. Françoise de Graffigny. *Letters from a Peruvian Woman.* Trans. David Kornacker. 1993.
3. Claire de Duras. *Ourika.* Trans. John Fowles. 1994.
4. Eleonore Thon. *Adelheit von Rastenberg.* Trans. George F. Peters. 1996.
5. Emilia Pardo Bazán. *"Torn Lace" and Other Stories.* Trans. María Cristina Urruela. 1996.

EMILIA PARDO BAZAN

Torn Lace
and Other Stories

Translated by
María Cristina Urruela

Introduction by
Joyce Tolliver

The Modern Language Association of America
New York   1996

For information about obtaining permission to reprint
material from MLA book publications, send your request by
mail (see address below), e-mail (permissions@mla.org), or
fax (212 533-0680).

Library of Congress Cataloging-in-Publication Data

Pardo Bazán, Emilia, condesa de, 1852–1921.
[Encaje roto y otros cuentos. English]
Torn lace and other stories / Emilia Pardo Bazán ;
translated by María Cristina Urruela ;
introduction by Joyce Tolliver.
p.   cm. — (Texts and translations.   Translations ; 5)
Includes bibliographical references (p.   ).
ISBN 0-87352-784-4 (pbk.)
I. Urruela, María Cristina, 1956–   . II. Title.   III. Series.
PQ6629.A7A613   1996
863'.5 — dc20   96-41223

ISSN 1079-2538

Set in Dante. Printed on recycled paper

Published by The Modern Language Association of America
10 Astor Place, New York, New York 10003-6981

CONTENTS

Contents

Acknowledgments

Many people have been of invaluable help to us in the preparation of this manuscript. We are especially indebted to Vern Williamsen and Florence Sandler, for reading every word of the manuscript in record time and for suggesting editorial changes that were all exactly right. Our thanks also go to Harriet Turner for her many wise suggestions and countless words of encouragement, to Robert Fedorchek for his expert editorial help and for graciously aiding us in securing copyright to the stories, and to Amy Williamsen for her constant support and creative vision. Alicia Andreu, Berta Aparicio, Flo Ariessohn, Maryellen Bieder, Curtis Blaylock, Iris Brest, Elena Delgado, Marisol Fernández Utrera, Consuelo García Devesa, Richard Halliburton, Paz Haro, Ignacio Hualde Mayo, Dana Livingston, Lisa Neal, Karen Offen, Michael Predmore, Don Share, Juan Francisco Urruela, Linda Wilhelm, and Martha Zárate helped us solve various problems, of translation and other types, and we are grateful to them for sharing their time and expertise. We would like to thank Ron Sousa and David Tinsley for their administrative and collegial support. Carlos Dorado Fernández, director of the Hemeroteca Municipal of Madrid, and Marino

Dónega of the Real Academia Gallega have our gratitude as well.

José Ignacio Hualde and Steven Stauss deserve special thanks for their constant willingness to serve as linguistic and cultural consultants and for listening, criticizing, and applauding, all at the appropriate moments.

Finally, we would like to thank Martha Evans for her efficiency, diplomacy, and perpetual good humor and optimism as she guided us through the intricacies of the review process.

This project was facilitated by support from the National Endowment for the Humanities; from the Department of Spanish, Italian, and Portuguese at the University of Illinois, Urbana; and from the Program for Cultural Cooperation between United States Universities and the Spanish Ministry of Culture.

MCU and JT

INTRODUCTION

Pardo Bazán, Writer and Intellectual

Emilia Pardo Bazán (1851–1921) is one of the most important literary figures of nineteenth-century Spain. She is without doubt the most influential Spanish woman writer of that century, instrumental in promoting an awareness of French naturalism and Russian spiritual realism in the Spanish reading public. Pardo Bazán singlehandedly authored and published an important journal, *Nuevo teatro crítico*, which appeared every month in 1891 and 1892. It served as a forum for her feminist ideas and included essays on philosophical, scientific, literary, and historical topics. Pardo Bazán also wrote an original story for practically every monthly issue. In addition to her novels, plays, poetry, and almost six hundred short stories, she wrote innumerable essays of social and literary criticism, which were published in the leading intellectual journals of her day.

She was born in La Coruña, Galicia, a province of northwestern Spain known for its mild, rainy climate and its Celtic influences, particularly those involving belief in the supernatural. Her parents were members of the gentry. As the only child, she enjoyed abundant encouragement and received a formal education that went far beyond the training in embroidery, piano, and French that was traditional for girls of her class at that time. According to her "Apuntes autobiográficos" (Autobiographical Notes),[1] her father opened his considerable library to her; she was allowed to read anything that interested her—with the exception of some French novels, which were widely considered to have a pernicious influence on young people and on women. At the age of fifteen, she married don José Quiroga y Pérez Deza, an eighteen-year-old law student. The marriage was arranged by the parents of the couple, although apparently neither Emilia nor José objected to the match (Bravo-Villasante 26–27). José encouraged Emilia to study his law books along with him, even though she was not allowed to attend classes (28). She even wrote class papers for him, which usually were assigned higher grades than his own.

Pardo Bazán first came to public attention as a writer in 1871, when she won a literary contest with an essay on the eighteenth-century writer Benito Jerónimo Feijóo, whom she admired for his feminist ideas. At the age of twenty-five she gave birth to her first child, Jaime, and had published her first collection of poetry. The collection, inspired by her son, bore his name as its title. Her first novel, *Pascual López, Autobiografía de un estudiante de medicina* (Pascual López, Autobiography of a Medical Student), was published in 1879; by 1881, when she published her second novel, *Un viaje de novios* (A Wedding Trip), she had begun to gain wide recognition as a novelist and intellectual.

It is difficult to classify Pardo Bazán's fictional writing in terms of literary movements. Most of her work clearly fits in the category of realism, some has strong Romantic overtones, and much of her later work is influenced by modernism and Russian spiritual realism. Although her fiction shows elements of various literary movements, she has come to be known primarily for her engagement with literary naturalism. She provoked considerable controversy among Spanish readers with her 1883 treatise *La cuestión palpitante* (The Burning Question), in which she describes and criticizes this literary and philosophical movement as propounded by its founder, the French novelist Emile Zola.

Stylistically, naturalism was influenced by the attempts of Auguste Comte to apply the methods of scientific observation to the social sciences, philosophy, and religion. The naturalists extended that application to literature. They attempted to re-create in their fiction the "experimental method" elaborated by the physician Claude Bernard. Naturalistic themes and plots were largely determined by Comte's positivistic philosophy, which emphasizes the importance of social change and improvement through scientific inquiry, and by the theories of Hippolyte Taine, who posited that each individual's life is inescapably determined by a combination of three factors: heredity, one's surroundings, and the historical moment in which one lives.

According to Pardo Bazán's critique, Zola's extreme interpretation of these theories is flawed because it ignores the strength of human spirituality, which can transcend such obstacles. Further, Pardo Bazán criticized his overly frequent depiction of the sordid, even the squalid, claiming that literature should make life more beautiful, not uglier. But her reading public tended to ignore her criticisms of Zola; it was scandalous that a woman should be reading Zola at all, much less commenting explicitly on him. In fact, José Quiroga, sharing the reaction of most of his wife's readers, demanded that she give up her writing career and dedicate herself to her marriage and her family. Pardo Bazán instead separated from her husband, set up household with her three children and her mother, and continued to write and publish for close to forty years more. Her fiction often demonstrates her own brand of attenuated naturalism. *Los pazos de Ulloa (The House of Ulloa)* is the novel most often cited as representative of her naturalism, although *La Tribuna* (The Woman Orator) and *La Madre Naturaleza* (Mother Nature) are also good examples.

By 1889, Pardo Bazán had firmly established herself as a presence in Spanish letters. In addition to her early book of poetry and her study of Feijóo, she had had published eight novels, a study of the Russian novel, two books of travel writing, a life of Saint Francis of Assisi, articles of literary criticism, essays on scientific advances, social commentary, and numerous short stories. When a seat was vacated in the Royal Spanish Academy, her name was mentioned in the discussion of a possible replacement. A polemic on the suitability of admitting a woman to the academy ensued, and the result was that Pardo Bazán was not granted this honor. She asserts that in more enlightened eras women did indeed hold seats in the several branches of the Royal Spanish Academy

("La cuestión" 201). She would never see a woman named to the Real Academia de la Lengua in her lifetime. It was not until 1979 that the academy named a woman, Carmen Conde, to its ranks.

It was clear to Pardo Bazán that the academy's exclusion of women was strictly a result of antiquated prejudice. She protested vigorously not only the academy's snubbing of her but also what she saw as the unjust exclusion of Gertrudis Gómez de Avellaneda a generation earlier. She later advocated the nomination of another woman writer, intellectual, and social reformer, Concepción Arenal. Although Pardo Bazán was accused of campaigning for Arenal merely to draw attention to her own cause, it is difficult to doubt the sincerity of her insistence that the "Academy question" was far more important than the question of her personal recognition and success, that it was a simple matter of sexual equity. In fact, Pardo Bazán had treated the many manifestations of sexual injustice in her fiction and essays before the academy polemic arose; she had portrayed the inadequate education given girls, sexual abuse in marriage, the difficulties faced by women of the working class, and, above all, the hypocrisy of sexual attitudes.

In an effort to facilitate access to fundamental feminist works, especially those in other languages, Pardo Bazán founded a book series called Biblioteca de la mujer (Woman's Library). This series included a translation of John Stuart Mill's *On the Subjection of Women* and August Bebel's *Die Frau und der Sozialismus (Woman under Socialism)* as well as modern versions of selected novellas of the seventeenth-century Spanish feminist María de Zayas y Sotomayor. More conventional works, such as a biography of Isabel la Católica (Queen Isabella) and a life of the Virgin Mary, were also included. However, by 1913 Pardo Bazán had become disillusioned and frustrated by the general lack of interest, in Spain, in feminism, among both men and women. She decided to publish two cookbooks, *La cocina española antigua* (Old-Fashioned Spanish Cuisine) and *La cocina española moderna* (Modern Spanish Cuisine), as the next volumes in the Woman's Library, explaining:

> I have seen, without a doubt, that here no one is interested in such matters, women even less so. . . . Here there are no suffragists, neither meek nor fierce. With this in mind, and because I don't want to fight a battle when no one cheers me on, I have decided to expand the Section of Home Economics of the said Library, and since it is useless to speak about women's rights and the advances women have made, I will pleasantly discuss the preparation of marinated partridge and almond sponge cake.[2]   (qtd. in Bravo-Villasante 285)

Fin-de-siècle Spain was simply not receptive to feminism, especially not to the fundamental feminism that formed the basis of Pardo Bazán's thought on sex roles. Pascual Santacruz's comments on what he termed "the age of the *marimacho*,"[3] published in 1907, illustrate the sort of opposition that Pardo Bazán had to confront:

> Feminism . . . is the tyranny imposed on those laws of nature that determine the psychological makeup of each sex. . . . Since the ideal that radical

> feminism pursues is the creation of the *marimacho*,
> and this *marimacho*, who tends more toward the
> masculine nature than the feminine, . . . is a thing
> which is itself grotesque, it can only be treated as
> a joke. . . . I will limit myself to chuckling along
> with those readers who think as I do (who must be
> in the majority) at this pathological manifestation,
> this raging rash on the body of society, which is
> harmless at first but soon becomes bothersome
> with its persistent itching.   (82–83)

These remarks come from a man who refers to Pardo
Bazán as his "illustrious friend and patroness" and who
regards her as unique among the women of her day in
her accomplishments and talent (88). When we consider
that such unself-conscious misogyny issued from a sup-
porter of Pardo Bazán and appeared in an important
journal, it is not difficult to imagine the resistance to her
feminism that Pardo Bazán must have encountered.

Indeed, even to a contemporary English-speaking audience many of her comments on "the woman question" seem remarkably forward-looking. But by no
means did Pardo Bazán's progressivism extend to all
spheres. She was a political conservative, and her writing
shows strong ambivalence on the question of social class.
While she often portrayed working-class and rural
women sympathetically in her fiction, she was far from
egalitarian; she defended the strict maintenance of class
hierarchy. Her personal life also shows a concern for social prestige and class dominance; over the course of
several years she dedicated considerable energy to the
acquisition of a title of nobility. After she finally achieved
this through papal decree, as had her father before her,

she invariably used the title of countess when signing her published work.

The political portrait of Pardo Bazán is made more complex by the fact that in a time of widespread anti-clericism among her contemporaries (e.g., Benito Pérez Galdós and Clarín) she called herself, to use her term, a devout "neo-Catholic." At the same time, she issued a piercing condemnation of the ways in which the church as an institution worked to control and restrict women. The following quotation, from "The Women of Spain,"[4] illustrates the mixture of stringent feminism, on the one hand, and classism and racism, on the other, that one often finds in this author:

> The man considers himself a superior being, authorized to throw off every yoke and question all authority and to arrange his life on an elastic moral system of his own making; but, influenced by the despotic and jealous temper natural to the African races, as he can no longer place a negro with a dagger in his girdle to watch over his wife, he gives her an august guardian, God! . . . Husbands, and all others who hold authority over women, know that the confessor is rather an ally than an enemy. It scarcely ever happens that the confessor advises a woman to protest, struggle, and emancipate herself, instead of submitting, yielding, and obeying.   (886)

Pardo Bazán was finally granted public recognition of her importance as a writer and intellectual in 1915, when the minister of public education, Julio Burell, created a professorship for her at the University of Madrid. She was the first woman to hold the position of professor (catedrático) in a Spanish university. When she was informed of this appointment, she paid a visit to the dean, requesting that he be sure to assign her a large classroom, as she had become accustomed to delivering speeches to audiences that filled lecture halls. At first she did indeed teach to a full classroom, but attendance soon dwindled, in part because her class was not required for any university degree. By the end of the course, according to one account (Sánchez Cantón 63–64), she lectured to a sole student, a distinguished and well-educated lady who happened to be a friend of hers. The story of Pardo Bazán's short teaching career is often cited to illustrate the opposition that existed in Spain then to the naming of a woman as a professor. But F. J. Sánchez Cantón adds a comment that puts Pardo Bazán's lack of students in a somewhat different light: "Don Ramón Menéndez Pidal had fewer than a dozen students, even though his courses were mandatory" (64).[5] Thus the very real opposition on the part of many of her male peers to her university appointment has been shifted, in traditional Pardo Bazán biography, to her anonymous students.

Pardo Bazán died 12 May 1921, at the age of sixty-nine. She had written 20 novels, 21 novellas, 2 cookbooks, 7 plays, at least 580 short stories, and hundreds of essays, not including the countless works that were dispersed among various periodicals and that have never been reprinted. Her eminence as a writer of fiction, essays, and literary criticism was universally recognized, even in her own day. While scholars have traditionally studied Pardo Bazán as a key figure in the Spanish naturalistic novel, they have recently begun to also recognize the fundamental contribution she made to Spanish letters through her experimentation with narrative structure and her exploration of other literary movements, such as spiritual realism and modernism. In addition, she is now credited with having played a major role in bringing the discussion of feminism to the forefront of intellectual and popular debate, through her fiction as well as through her essays.

The Stories

Despite the remarkable number of short stories that Pardo Bazán wrote (or perhaps because the sheer number of them is so daunting), critics have overwhelmingly preferred to direct their attention to her novels. Yet Pardo Bazán is generally considered to be one of the two most important short story writers of nineteenth-century Spain. Only Leopoldo Alas (Clarín) is comparable to her in stylistic skill and diversity, and he wrote only about sixty stories. Pardo Bazán is often compared with Maupassant in her command of this genre, and her stories are routinely anthologized. Translations of them, however, have been curiously scarce, in keeping with the general dearth of English-language versions of her work. The bulk of English translations of her work was published between 1891 and 1929. Between 1929 and 1993, only a half dozen English translations appeared. Two of them, published recently and within a year of each other, are of the novel *Los pazos de Ulloa* (*The House of Ulloa*); the other four are stories included in anthologies. An anthology of stories by Pardo Bazán in English translation did not appear until 1993: *"The White Horse" and Other Stories,* translated by Robert M. Fedorchek. While necessarily containing only a small percentage of the stories, this collection ably represents their thematic and stylistic heterogeneity.

Pardo Bazán's stories are usually included in anthologies to exemplify her naturalism. But the interest these texts hold for the contemporary scholar and the casual reader alike goes beyond her rather ambivalent involvement with this literary movement. Naturalism is far from the only stylistic mode found in her fiction. Maurice Hemingway has shown that many literary currents are reflected in Pardo Bazán's work and that most of the novels have been influenced by more than one movement. This is true of the stories as well; they contain not only naturalism but also psychological realism, spiritual realism, modernism, decadentism, and even some engagement—if antagonistic—with Romanticism. What is more striking than the diversity is the convergence of literary currents within many of the individual stories.

The stories show great subtlety in their portrayal of human psychology and a highly sophisticated use of narrative structure, anticipating the modernist short story of such later writers in English as Katherine Mansfield and Virginia Woolf. Many of Pardo Bazán's stories revolve around the modernist notion of epiphany, in which a seemingly minor event leads the protagonist to a sudden realization of an important truth. Others are notable for a quick, compact development of plot and characterization that culminates in a surprise ending—the surprise residing not in a plot twist but in an unexpected interpretation of everything that led up to it. That most of Pardo Bazán's stories are quite short makes her sophisticated play with narrative perspective all the more remarkable. Rarely do her stories have only one narrative perspective; they usually contain several subtle shifts, which are signaled only by a change or an anomaly in verb tense or by an alteration in dialect or register.

As Juan Paredes Núñez, Mariano Baquero Goyanes, and others have demonstrated, one finds in Pardo Bazán's short stories a wide variety of themes. Paredes Núñez's classification of her stories, which largely follows Baquero Goyanes's, gives the following seven categories: religious stories, patriotic and social stories, psychological stories (including stories about love), stories about Galicia, dramatic and tragic stories, popular stories involving fantasy and legend, and stories about "small objects and beings." Several categories could be added to this list—detective stories, stories written for holidays and other special occasions, hagiographic stories, and, of course, feminist stories.

Thematically, many of Pardo Bazán's stories bear a striking relevance to contemporary concerns, especially those concerns having to do with the relationships between men and women. It is in the stories more than in the novels that one finds a thorough and multifaceted development of her ideas regarding gender dynamics. She treats issues that now, a century later, form the basis of much feminist discourse. These include the nature of female sexuality and desire ("Memento," "Champagne," "The Wedding," "The Look," "The Pink Tree"); male dominance, both physical and psychological ("Piña,"

"Sister Aparición," "Feminist," "The Cigarette Stub," "The Wedding," "The Look"); the double standard ("The Forewarned," "Champagne," "Sister Aparición"); and the relation between poverty and gender roles ("Castaways," "Champagne"). In stories like "Feminist," "The Key," "Piña," and "The Oldest Story," Pardo Bazán attacks from several different angles the sexual ideal that posits female abnegation and submission not only as virtuous but as expressive of feminine nature. "The Oldest Story" is particularly modern in its feminist re-vision of the story of Adam and Eve; it suggests that women's submission to male authority is by no means divinely ordained but rather a result of the conditioning women receive from the patriarchal culture.

Many of Pardo Bazán's stories portray marriages and weddings ("Torn Lace," "Champagne," "Feminist," "The Wedding," "The Cigarette Stub," "The Key"). Thomas Feeny has commented on the "pessimistic view of love" in stories like these, but perhaps there is more to the matter than simple personal pessimism. Marriage, both as a social institution and as a personal relationship, is an ideal object of study for an author like Pardo Bazán, who is interested in exploring the intricacies of human psychology as well as the complex interplay between power and desire that is integral to relationships between men and women in most cultures. Indeed, only two of the six stories mentioned in this paragraph suggest the possibility for a happy, healthy union beween husband and wife, and in both the suggestion is highly ambiguous. More to the point, in each of the six stories we find an implicit interrogation of some aspect of gender dynamics as they are captured and crystallized in the marriage.

The sixteen stories of this collection represent feminist themes that recur consistently in Pardo Bazán's stories. Most were published between 1890 and 1914, the period during which Pardo Bazán was most active as a feminist and as a short story writer. Since they touch on more than one theme, I have chosen to present them chronologically rather than group them thematically. Each of the tales is preceded by a short introduction.

These stories were selected not only for their thematic development but also for the ways in which, taken as a group, they suggest the rich stylistic variety and narrative complexity of Pardo Bazán's short fiction. Their chronological ordering shows how the author's stylistic concerns and alliances changed over the years; at the same time it allows us to see how the stylistic germs of the later stories are present in the earlier ones. Three early stories, "First Love," "My Suicide," and "Sister Aparición," lampoon some of the gendered conventions of Romanticism. By the time Pardo Bazán wrote her last story, "The Pink Tree," her style had moved considerably closer to the modernist attempt to "capture the moment." But we find this modernist characteristic in earlier stories as well, such as "Torn Lace" and "The Forewarned." Similarly, the stark naturalism present in "Piña" is sharpened and polished in "Castaways," published nineteen years later.

I have borrowed the title of one of the stories for the title of this collection because "Torn Lace" seems to epitomize Pardo Bazán's thematic and stylistic presentation of the cultural construct of femininity. The image evoked by this title not only indicates the writer's rejection of patriarchal sexual and social mores; it also draws attention to the complexity of her textual artistry, with its simultaneous evocation and subversion of "the feminine."

Notes

[1] Titles of works that exist in English translation are in italics or enclosed in quotation marks. (See the bibliographic section following the introduction.) Titles that are neither in italics nor enclosed in quotation marks do not exist in English translation.

[2] All translations from the Spanish are mine, unless otherwise indicated. The ellipsis here does not indicate missing text; it follows the punctuation of the original. The following quotation from Santacruz, however, contains genuine ellipses.

[3] The word *marimacho*, highly pejorative, combines the feminine *mari*, from *María*, with *macho* to denote an inappropriately masculine woman.

[4] This essay first appeared in English, in the *Fortnightly Review* (1889). A year later, Pardo Bazán published a slightly longer version of the essay in Spanish. No translator is credited for the *Fortnightly Review* essay.

[5] Ramón Menéndez Pidal (1869–1968) is still considered one of the greatest figures in Spanish philology.

Works Cited and Consulted

Baquero Goyanes, Mariano. *El cuento español en el siglo XIX.* Madrid: Consejo Superior de Investigaciones Científicas, 1949.

Bravo-Villasante, Carmen. *Vida y obra de Emilia Pardo Bazán: Correspondencia amorosa con Pérez Galdós.* Madrid: Magisterio Español, 1973.

Feeny, Thomas. "Pardo Bazán's Pessimistic View of Love As Revealed in *Cuentos de amor.*" *Hispanófila* 64 (1978): 7–14.

Hemingway, Maurice. *Emilia Pardo Bazán: The Making of a Novelist.* Cambridge: Cambridge UP, 1983.

Osborne, Robert E. *Emilia Pardo Bazán: Su vida y sus obras.* Mexico: Andrea, 1964.

Pardo Bazán, Emilia. "Apuntes autobiográficos." Prologue to *Los pazos de Ulloa.* Barcelona: Cortezo, 1886. Rpt. in *Obras completas.* Vol. 3. Ed. Harry L. Kirby. Madrid: Aguilar, 1973. 698–732.

———. "La cuestión académica." *"La mujer española" y otros artículos feministas.* Ed. Leda Schiavo. Madrid: Nacional, 1976. 197–204.

———. *"The White Horse" and Other Stories.* Ed. and trans. Robert M. Fedorchek. Lewisburg: Bucknell UP, 1993.

———. "The Women of Spain." *Fortnightly Review* 1 June 1889: 879–904.

Paredes Núñez, Juan. *Los cuentos de Emilia Pardo Bazán.* Granada: U de Granada, 1979.

Pattison, Walter. *Emilia Pardo Bazán.* New York: Twayne, 1971.

Sánchez Cantón, F. J. "Doña Emilia Pardo Bazán en la Facultad." *El centenario de doña Emilia Pardo Bazán.* Madrid: Facultad de filosofía y letras, U de Madrid, 1952. 58–65.

Santacruz, Pascual. "El siglo de los marimachos." *La España moderna* 19 (1907): 79–94.

BIBLIOGRAPHY

About the Author

Bravo-Villasante, Carmen. *Vida y obra de Emilia Pardo Bazán.* Madrid: Revista de Occidente, 1962.

————. *Vida y obra de Emilia Pardo Bazán: Correspondencia amorosa con Pérez Galdós.* Madrid: Magisterio Español, 1973.

Osborne, Robert E. *Emilia Pardo Bazán: Su vida y sus obras.* Mexico: Andrea, 1964.

Pardo Bazán, Emilia. "Apuntes autobiográficos." Prologue to *Los pazos de Ulloa.* Barcelona: Cortezo, 1886. Rpt. in *Obras completas.* Vol. 3. Ed. Harry L. Kirby. Madrid: Aguilar, 1973. 698–732.

Pattison, Walter. *Emilia Pardo Bazán.* New York: Twayne, 1971.

Sánchez Cantón, F. J. "Doña Emilia Pardo Bazán en la Facultad." *El centenario de doña Emilia Pardo Bazán.* Madrid: Facultad de filosofía y letras, U de Madrid, 1952. 58–65.

Works by Emilia Pardo Bazán—in Spanish

All except the collection of essays *"La mujer española" y otros artículos feministas* are included in the Aguilar *Obras completas.*

MAJOR NOVELS

El cisne de Vilamorta (1885)
Una cristiana (1890)
Dulce dueño (1911)
Insolación (1889)
La Madre Naturaleza (1887)
Memorias de un solterón (1896)
Morriña (1889)
Los pazos de Ulloa (1886)
La prueba (1890)
La quimera (1905)
La sirena negra (1908)
La Tribuna (1882)
Un viaje de novios (1881)

SELECTED ESSAYS

Al pie de la Torre Eiffel, por Francia y por Alemania (1889)
La cuestión palpitante (1883)
"La mujer española" y otros artículos feministas (1890–93)
La revolución y la novela en Rusia (1887)

SHORT STORY COLLECTIONS

Compiled by the Author in Her 44-Volume *Obras completas*

Cuentos de amor. Vol. 16. Madrid: Prieto, 1898.
Cuentos de la tierra. Vol. 43. Madrid: Atlántida, 1922.
Cuentos de Marineda. Vol. 5. Madrid: Pueyo, 1892.
Cuentos de Navidad y Reyes; Cuentos de la Patria; Cuentos antiguos.
  Vol. 25. Madrid: Pueyo, 1902.
Cuentos nuevos. Vol. 10. Madrid: Prieto, 1894.
Cuentos sacroprofanos. Vol. 17. Madrid: Prieto, 1899.
Un destripador de antaño: Historias y cuentos regionales. Vol. 2.
  Madrid: Prieto, 1900.

En tranvía: Cuentos dramáticos. Vol. 23. Madrid: Renacimiento, 1901.

El fondo del alma: Cuentos del terruño. Vol. 31. Madrid: Prieto, 1907.

Sudexprés. Vol. 36. Madrid: Pueyo, 1909.

Compiled by Others

Kirby, Harry L., ed. *Obras completas.* Vol. 3. Madrid: Aguilar, 1973.

Paredes Núñez, Juan, ed. *Cuentos completos.* 4 vols. La Coruña: Fundación Pedro Barrie de la Maza, Conde de Fenosa, 1990.

————. *Los cuentos de Emilia Pardo Bazán.* Granada: U de Granada, 1979.

————, ed. *Cuentos: Selección.* Madrid: Taurus, 1984.

Sainz de Robles, Federico, ed. *Obras completas.* Vols. 1 and 2. Madrid: Aguilar, 1957.

Works by Emilia Pardo Bazán—in English

NOVELS

The Angular Stone. Trans. of *La piedra angular.* Trans. Mary J. Serrano. New York: Cassell, 1892; Merson 1900. Excerpted in *Contemporary Spain As Shown by Her Novelists.* Ed. Mary Wright Plummer. New York: Truslove, 1899.

A Christian Woman. Trans. of *Una cristiana.* Trans. Mary A. Springer. New York: Cassell, 1891. Excerpted in *Contemporary Spain As Shown by Her Novelists.* Ed. Mary Wright Plummer. New York: Truslove, 1899.

The House of Ulloa. Trans. of *Los pazos de Ulloa.* Trans. Paul O'Prey and Lucia Graves. New York: Penguin, 1991.

The House of Ulloa. Trans. Roser Caminals-Heath. Athens: U of Georgia P, 1992.

Midsummer Madness. Trans. of *Insolación.* Trans. Amparo Loring. Boston: Clark, 1907.

Morriña (Homesickness). Trans. Mary J. Serrano. New York: Cassell, 1891. Excerpted in *Contemporary Spain As Shown by Her Novelists*. Ed. Mary Wright Plummer. New York: Truslove, 1899.

The Mystery of the Lost Dauphin (Louis XVII). Trans. of *Misterio*. Trans. Annabel Hord Seeger. New York: Funk, 1906.

The Son of the Bondswoman. Trans. of *Los pazos de Ulloa*. Trans. Ethel Harriet Hearn. New York: n.p., 1908. New York: Fertig, 1976.

The Swan of Vilamorta. Trans. of *El cisne de Vilamorta*. Trans. Mary J. Serrano. New York: Cassell, 1891. Excerpted in *Contemporary Spain As Shown by Her Novelists*. Ed. Mary Wright Plummer. New York: Truslove, 1899.

A Wedding Trip. Trans. of *Un viaje de novios*. Trans. Mary J. Serrano. New York: Cassell, 1891; Chicago: Hennebury, 1910.

ESSAYS

Russia, Its People and Its Literature. Trans. of *La revolución y la novela en Rusia*. Trans. Fanny Hale Gardiner. Chicago: McClurg, 1901.

"The Women of Spain." Trans. of "La mujer española." *Fortnightly Review* 1 June 1889: 879–904.

STORIES

"A Churchman Militant." Trans. of "Nieto del Cid." *Tales from the Italian and Spanish*. Vol. 8. New York: Review, 1920. 92–100. *"A Moral Divorce" and Other Stories of Modern Spain*. Ed. E. Haldeman-Julius. Little Blue Book 1197. Girard: Haldeman-Julius, 1927. 37–48.

"First Love." Trans. of "Primer amor." *Tales from the Italian and Spanish*. Vol. 8. New York: Review, 1920. 273–80. *"First Love" and Other Fascinating Stories of Spanish Life*. Ed. E. Haldeman-Julius. Little Blue Book 1195. Girard: Haldeman-Julius, 1927. 5–14.

"First Prize." Trans. of "El premio gordo." Trans. Armando Zegri. *Great Stories of All Nations*. New York: Brentano's, 1927. 209–14.

"The Heart Lover." Trans. of "Un destripador de antaño." Trans. Edward and Elizabeth Huberman. *Great Spanish Short Stories*. Ed. Angel Flores. New York: Dell, 1962. 114–38.

"The Last Will of Don Javier." Trans. of "Desde allá." *Tales from the Italian and Spanish*. Vol. 8. New York: Review, 1920. 267–72.

"The Pardon." Trans. of "El indulto." *Tales from the Italian and Spanish*. Vol. 8. New York: Review, 1920. 215–25. *"The Devil's Mother-in-Law" and Other Stories of Modern Spain*. Ed. E. Haldeman-Julius. Little Blue Book 1198. Girard: Haldeman-Julius, 1927. 30–43.

"The Revolver." Trans. of "El revólver." Trans. Angel Flores. *Spanish Stories: Cuentos españoles*. New York: Bantam, 1960. 116–27.

"Sister Aparición." Trans. of "Sor Aparición." Trans. Harriet de Onís. *Spanish Stories and Tales*. New York: Knopf, 1954. 90–95.

"The Talisman." Trans. of "El talismán." Trans. William E. Colford. *Classic Tales from Modern Spain*. Great Neck: Barron's, 1964. 24–32.

"The White Horse" and Other Stories. Trans. Robert M. Fedorchek. Lewisburg: Bucknell UP, 1993.

Selected Criticism on the Stories

Ashworth, Peter P. "Of Spinning Wheels and Witches: Pardo Bazán's 'Afra' and *La bruja*." *Letras femeninas* 18.1–2 (1992): 108–18.

Baquero Goyanes, Mariano. *El cuento español: Del romanticismo al realismo*. Ed. Ana L. Baquero Escudero. Madrid: Consejo Superior de Investigaciones Científicas, 1992.

———. *El cuento español en el siglo XIX.* Madrid: Consejo Superior de Investigaciones Científicas, 1949.

Cannon, Harold L. "Algunos aspectos estilísticos en los cuentos de Emilia Pardo Bazán." *Káñina* 7.2 (1983): 83–92.

Cate-Arries, Francie. "Murderous Impulses and Moral Ambiguity: Emilia Pardo Bazán's Crime Stories." *Romance Quarterly* 39 (1992): 205–10.

Charnon-Deutsch, Lou. "Naturalism in the Short Fiction of Emilia Pardo Bazán." *Hispanic Journal* 3 (1981): 73–85.

———. *The Nineteenth-Century Spanish Story: Textual Strategies of a Genre in Transition.* London: Tamesis, 1985.

Durham, Carolyn Richardson. "Subversion in Two Short Stories by Emilia Pardo Bazán." *Letras peninsulares* 2 (1989): 55–64.

Eberenz, Rolf. *Semiótica y morfología textual del cuento naturalista: E. Pardo Bazán, L. Alas "Clarín," V. Blasco Ibáñez.* Madrid: Gredos, 1989.

Feeny, Thomas. "Illusion and the Don Juan Theme in Pardo Bazán's *Cuentos de amor.*" *Hispanic Journal* 1.11 (1980): 67–71.

González Torres, Rafael. *Los cuentos de Emilia Pardo Bazán.* Boston: Florentia, 1977.

Livingston, Dana J. "The Subversion of Sexual and Gender Roles in the Short Fiction of Emilia Pardo Bazán." Diss. U of Colorado, 1995.

Paredes Núñez, Juan. "El cuento policíaco en Pardo Bazán." *Estudios sobre literatura y arte dedicados al profesor Emilio Orozco Díaz.* Vol. 3. Granada: U de Granada, 1979. 7–18.

———. *Los cuentos de Emilia Pardo Bazán.* Granada: U de Granada, 1979.

Pérez, Janet. "Winners, Losers, and Casualties in Pardo Bazán's Battle of the Sexes." *Letras peninsulares* 5 (1992–93): 347–56.

Rey, Alfonso. "El cuento psicológico en Pardo Bazán." *Hispanófila* 59 (1977): 19–30.

Sánchez, Porfirio. "How and Why Emilia Pardo Bazán Went from the Novel to the Short Story." *Romance Notes* 11 (1969): 309–14.

Tolliver, Joyce. "Knowledge, Desire, and Syntactic Empathy in Pardo Bazán's 'La novia fiel.'" *Hispania* 72 (1989): 909–18.

———. "'La Que Entrega La Mirada, Lo Entrega Todo': The Sexual Economy of the Gaze in Pardo Bazán's 'La mirada.'" *Romance Languages Annual* 4 (1993): 620–26.

———. "Script Theory, Perspective, and Message in Narrative: The Case of 'Mi suicidio.'" *The Text and Beyond: Essays in Literary Linguistics*. Ed. Cynthia Goldin Bernstein. Tuscaloosa: U of Alabama P, 1994. 97–119.

———. "'Sor Aparición' and the Gaze: Pardo Bazán's Gendered Reply to the Romantic Don Juan." *Hispania* 77 (1994): 185–96.

NOTE ON EDITIONS

Most of Pardo Bazán's stories appeared in at least two forms during her lifetime. They were first published in periodicals intended for a general public, or occasionally in literary journals, and were then included in the author's self-compiled *Obras completas*, published in forty-four volumes between 1891 and 1922. Pardo Bazán often made editorial changes when preparing the stories for publication in her *Obras completas*. For this reason, while we consulted the original journal publication to identify any important authorial revisions that might affect the stories' interpretation, the translations that follow are based on the later version.

Pardo Bazán, like many of her contemporaries, used punctuation, especially ellipses, in an idiosyncratic way. Wherever possible, we have retained the punctuation as well as the paragraph division of the self-compiled *Obras completas*.

The reader who wishes to consult other stories by Pardo Bazán in their original Spanish may also find them in contemporary versions. Juan Paredes Núñez has united 580 of the stories in his four-volume *Cuentos completos*, although in the introduction to the first volume he admits that it is highly likely that there are still more, unedited, stories by this author. His collection has several useful appendixes, including one that lists the original publication data for each story. Most of the stories found in Paredes Núñez's edition are included in the three-volume *Obras completas* of Pardo Bazán published by Aguilar in 1957 (vols. 1 and 2) and 1973 (vol. 3). The original publication information for the stories included in this volume is as follows:

"Primer amor." *Revista ibérica* 14, 1883; *La dama joven y otros cuentos.* (Barcelona: Cortezo, 1885); *Cuentos de amor.*

"Piña." *La ilustración artística* 447, 1890; *Cuentos nuevos.*

"Cuento primitivo." *El imparcial,* 7 Aug. 1893; *Cuentos nuevos.*

"Mi suicidio." *El imparcial,* 12 Mar. 1894; *Cuentos de amor.*

"Sor Aparición." *El imparcial,* 19 Sep. 1896; *Cuentos de amor.*

"Memento." *El imparcial,* 20 Apr. 1896; *Cuentos de amor.*

"El encaje roto." *El liberal,* 19 Sep. 1897; *Cuentos de amor.*

"Champagne." *Cuentos de amor.*

"La mirada." *El imparcial,* 7 Dec. 1908; *Sudexprés.*

"La clave." *Blanco y negro* 914, 1908; *Sudexprés.*

"La boda." *Sudexprés.*

"Los escarmentados." *Sudexprés.*

"Náufragas." *Blanco y negro* 946, 1909; *Cuentos nuevos.*

"Feminista." *Sudexprés.*

"La punta del cigarro." *La ilustración española y americana,* 36, 30 Sep. 1914.

"El árbol rosa." *Raza española,* special issue dedicated to the memory of Pardo Bazán, 1921.

Cuentos de amor. Obras completas. Vol. 16 (Madrid: Prieto, 1898).

Cuentos nuevos. Obras completas. Vol. 10 (Madrid: Prieto, 1894).

Sudexprés. Obras completas. Vol. 36 (Madrid: Pueyo, 1909).

Torn Lace
and Other Stories

FIRST LOVE

"First Love" repeats a common theme and has the structure of many other stories, such as Turgenev's First Love *(1860), that develop this theme: a mature male narrator recounts to a group of male friends his first amorous adventure. Pardo Bazán's version offers a subtly gendered difference, however, in the ironic inclusion of the voice of the female object of desire at the story's end. Her wry twist of the classic* vanitas *theme offsets the grotesque element of the narrator's description of the woman's aged body. Pardo Bazán often lampoons Romantic clichés, but "First Love" does this gently and perhaps even poignantly.*

How old was I back then? Eleven or twelve? Probably thirteen, because before thirteen it's too early to fall so deeply in love; but I dare not swear to anything, given that in southern countries the heart, if indeed that organ can be blamed for causing such emotional upheavals, gets off to an early start.

But if I can't remember *when* too well, at least I can say with complete certainty *how* my passion began to reveal itself. After my aunt went off to church for her morning devotions, I loved slipping into her bedroom and turning

3

the admirably well-ordered drawers of her bureau inside out. For me those drawers were a museum. I always stumbled upon something old and unusual in them, something that exhaled an archaic and distinct fragrance—the sandalwood from the fans that were scattered around to perfume the linens; pincushions of long-discolored satin; fingerless mesh gloves folded up between sheets of tissue paper; holy pictures; sewing accessories; a blue velvet reticule embroidered with silver thread; an amber-and-silver rosary—these all appeared in various corners. I examined each with curiosity and returned it to its place. But one day—I remember it as if it were today—in the corner of the top drawer I saw the glint of a golden object through some age-worn lace collars. I thrust my hands in, unwittingly crumpling the lace, and withdrew a portrait, a miniature on ivory probably no more than three inches tall and encased in a gold frame.

I stood enthralled as I gazed at it. A ray of sunlight filtered through the windowpane, striking the seductive image, which seemed to want to detach itself from its dark background and come toward me. She was an exquisite creature, one such as I had beheld only in my adolescent dreams, when the first shivers of puberty filled me with vague sorrows and undefinable yearnings whenever dusk fell.

The lady in the portrait was perhaps a little over

4

twenty; she was not a maiden, a half-open bud, but a woman in the full bloom of her beauty. She had an oval face that was not too long; full, round lips open in a smile; her heavily lidded eyes gazed languidly; and the dimple on her chin seemed to have been formed by Cupid's playful fingertip. Her hair was unusual but pleasing: a compact cluster of curls over her temples, and on top of her head braids interwoven like a basket. This old-fashioned hairstyle—tucked in at the nape of the neck—revealed all the softness of her youthful throat, where the dimple on her chin was repeated, but more delicately. Now her dress . . . I can't decide whether our grandmothers were intrinsically less discreet than our wives are or whether confessors of olden days were more broad-minded than confessors now; I tend to believe the latter, because sixty years ago women certainly took pride in being devout Christians, and they wouldn't have disobeyed their spiritual advisers in such serious and public matters. But there is no doubt that if a woman today went out dressed like the woman in the portrait, she would create a scene, since above the waist, beginning almost under her arms, she was veiled only by a light, undulating, diaphanous gauze, which accentuated rather than hid two scandalous snowy peaks. A thread of pearls snaked in between these peaks, before coming to rest on the shiny surface of the satiny décolletage. With similar immodesty she displayed her round arms, worthy of Juno, that ended in finely sculptured hands . . . When I say hands, I am not being exact, because strictly speaking I saw only one hand, it holding tightly a magnificent handkerchief.

To this day I marvel at how intensely I was struck in contemplating that miniature and how I became entranced as I breathlessly devoured the portrait with my eyes. I had seen prints of beautiful women before: in the *Ilustraciones,*[1] in the mythological engravings in the dining room, in store windows. It happened often that my precociously artistic eyes were captivated by a charming figure, a harmonious and elegant contour; but I imagined that the miniature found in my aunt's drawer, aside from its great gentility, was endowed with a subtle and vital aura. It was obvious that this was not some painter's whim but rather the image of a real person, flesh and blood, the genuine article. The rich and succulent tone of the impasto brought out the warm blood that lay beneath the pearl-colored skin; the lips parted to reveal the enamel of her teeth; and, to complete the illusion, there curled around the frame a border of wavy, silken auburn hair that had once grown on the temples of the painting's actual subject. I repeat: this was more

---

[1] Illustrated weekly magazines, designed for a general audience.

than a copy, this was a reflection of a real person, from whom I was separated only by glass cover . . . I lay my hand on it, warmed it with my breath, and the warmth of the mysterious deity seemed to flow to my lips and course through my veins. In the midst of this, I caught the sound of footsteps in the hallway. It was my aunt returning from her prayers. I heard her asthmatic cough and the shuffling of her gouty feet. I barely had time to drop the miniature back into the drawer, close it, and move to the window, where I adopted a nonchalant, innocent pose.

My aunt came in blowing her nose loudly, for the chill of the church had worsened her chronic cold. When she saw me, her reddened little eyes grew animated, and, giving me a friendly pat with her withered palm, she asked me whether I had been going through her drawers, as was my custom.

Then, with a chuckle, she added:

"Wait a second, wait a second. I have something for you that will make you lick your chops . . ."

From her ample handbag she took a packet, and from the packet three or four gumdrops that were stuck together, half squashed. They filled me with disgust.

The sight of my aunt certainly didn't invite one to open up and gobble down the candy: she was terribly old; her teeth were worn, her eyes were much too weak to be useful; there were hints of a mustache or bristle above her sunken mouth; on her yellowed temples dirty gray hair went every which way, divided with a three-finger-wide part; and her neck was as flaccid and livid as the wattles of a turkey in a good mood. So I wouldn't take the gumdrops. Ugh! A feeling of indignation rose within me, a manly protest, and I energetically declared:

"I don't want them, I don't want them!"

"You don't want them? What a wonder! And you with that sweet tooth of yours!"

"I'm not a little boy anymore," I exclaimed, trying to make myself taller, standing on the tips of my toes. "And I don't like sweets."

My aunt looked at me half kindly and half ironically, but at last gave in to her amusement and burst out laughing, which disfigured her even more, emphasizing the frightful anatomy of her jowls. She laughed so heartily that her chin and nose bumped together and hid her lips. Two wrinkles—or, rather, two deep furrows—and more than a dozen folds on her cheeks and eyelids stood out prominently. At the same time, her chest and head rocked with convulsive laughter, finally interrupted by a cough. Between guffaws and coughing fits, the old lady involuntarily sprayed my face with a shower of saliva. Humiliated and disgusted, I fled the scene, not stopping until I reached my mother's room, where I washed with soap and water and turned my thoughts to the lady in the portrait.

From that moment on, I was unable to drag my thoughts from her. As soon as my aunt left, I would slip into the room, open the drawer, and take out the miniature, enraptured by it. By dint of looking at it in this way, I imagined that her upturned eyes, gazing through the voluptuous shadows of her lashes, were fixed on mine and that her white bosom heaved passionately. It became embarrassing to kiss her because I fancied that she was angry at my brazenness, and so I merely pressed her against my heart or held my face close to hers. All my thoughts and actions revolved around the lady; I fussed and fretted over her, even to the smallest details. Before entering my aunt's room and opening the coveted drawer, I washed, combed my hair, and tidied myself up—as one does, I later learned, before an amorous rendezvous.

It often happened that I would run into boys my age, who were already provided with angelic little girlfriends. They proudly showed me letters, portraits, and flowers, asking me when I too would choose *my girl* to exchange love letters with. An inexplicable modesty tied my tongue, and I answered them only with a proud and enigmatic smile. When they asked for my opinion of the beauty of their damsels, I shrugged my shoulders and disdainfully rated them as *awful frights*. One Sunday it happened that I went to play at the home of several of my female cousins, really very charming girls, the eldest of whom couldn't have been fifteen. We were entertained by looking through a stereoscope, when suddenly one of the girls—the youngest, who counted twelve summers at most—furtively took my hand and, filled with emotion, red as a strawberry, whispered:

"Here, take this!"

At that moment I felt something soft and cool in the palm of my hand, and saw that it was a rosebud with its green leaves. The little girl withdrew, smiling and casting a sidelong glance at me; but I, with a puritanism worthy of the chaste Joseph, shouted in turn:

"Take this!"

And I threw the bud in her face—a rebuff that made her weepy and cross with me all afternoon, and that she probably still hasn't forgiven me for, even now that she is married and has three children.

I came to think that the two or three hours I had in the middle of each afternoon for admiring the portrait while my aunt was at church were too short, and so I finally resolved to put the miniature in my pocket, and all day I would hide from people as though I had committed a crime. I fancied that the portrait was witness to all my actions from the depths of its cloth prison, and I went to such extremes that if I wanted to scratch an itch, pull up a sock, or do anything else that didn't conform to the ideals of my most pristine love, I took the miniature out and deposited it in a safe place—and only then considered myself free to do as I pleased. In short, since carrying out the theft, I was possessed; at night I hid the portrait under my pillow and fell asleep in a position of defense, the portrait next to the wall, I on the outside. A thousand times I woke, fearing someone would come to snatch my treasure away. Finally I removed it from under the pillow and slipped it between my shirt and skin, on my left nipple, where the imprints of the chiseled ornaments of the frame were visible the next morning.

This contact with the beloved miniature made for delicious dreams. The lady in the portrait came toward me—not in effigy but in her natural size and proportions, live, graceful, affable, elegant, to take me to her palace in a carriage with soft cushions. With sweet authority she made me sit on a pillow at her feet, and she moved her shapely hand over my head, caressing my forehead, my eyes, and my tousled hair. I read to her from a large missal or played the lute, and she deigned to smile at me, thanking me for the pleasure my songs and readings gave her. In short, all manner of romantic thoughts boiled in my brain. I was now a page, now a troubadour.

In the midst of all these fantasies, the fact was that I was visibly losing weight, and my parents and aunt observed this with great anxiety.

"In this difficult and critical period of development, everything is alarming," said my father, who was accustomed to reading medical books, as he suspiciously took note of my dimmed eyes, the dark circles under them, my pale and tense mouth, and especially the complete lack of appetite that had taken hold of me.

"Play, my son; eat, my son," they would say to me.

And I would answer, subdued, "I don't care to."

They began to think of distractions for me; they offered to take me to the theater, they stopped my studies, and they gave me milk to drink, frothy and fresh from the cow's udder. Then they doused my neck and back with showers of cold water to fortify my nerves. I noticed that my father, at the table or in the mornings when I went to his room to wish him a good morning, stared at me awhile; sometimes he would slide his hands down my spine, palpating and probing my vertebrae. Hypocritically I would lower my eyes, resolved to die before confessing to my crime. As soon as I rid myself of my family's loving inspection, I was back again with my lady of the portrait. Finally, to get as close as possible to her, I decided to remove the cold glass. I hesitated before carrying this out, but in the end my love was stronger than the fear inspired in me by such a desecration, and with great dexterity I managed to pull off the glass and bring the ivory panel into clear view.

When I touched my lips to the painting and smelled the tenuous fragrance of the hair braid around the edge, I imagined with even more certainty that I held the living person in my trembling grasp. A feeling of faintness overpowered me, and I lay on the sofa as if unconscious, clutching the miniature.

When I came to my senses, I saw my father, my mother, and my aunt bending over me anxiously, fear and surprise in their faces. My father took my pulse, shook his head, and murmured:

"His pulse is a trickle, it's barely there."

My aunt, with her gnarled fingers, tried to take the portrait away from me, but mechanically I hid it and held on to it all the more.

"Dear boy . . . let go of it. You'll ruin it!" she exclaimed. "Can't you see you're smudging it? I'm not scolding you, boy, I'll show it to you as often as you like. But don't ruin it. Let go, you're damaging it."

"Let him have it," my mother entreated. "The boy is sick."

"That's all I need!" the old maid answered. "Give it up! And who will make another one like this? Who will take me back to those days? Nobody paints miniatures nowadays . . . that's a thing of the past, and so am I. I'm no longer what you see there."

My eyes dilated in horror; my fingers loosened their grip on the painting. I don't know how I managed to utter:

"You . . . the portrait . . . it's you . . . ?"

"I don't seem so beautiful to you now, little boy? Bah! Twenty-six years are prettier than . . . than . . . than I don't know how many, because I'm not keeping track. Nobody is going to steal them from me!"

My head drooped, and I must have fainted again, because my father carried me in his arms to bed and made me drink some spoonfuls of port wine.

I regained my health quickly and I refused ever again to enter my aunt's room.

PIÑA

*In the clearly implied parallels between the behavior of the
monkeys Piña and Coco and that of human beings, Pardo
Bazán allies herself with the naturalist view of human life
as governed primarily by animal instincts. But at the same
time, the animal-human behavior she chooses to represent—Piña's passive acceptance of her mate's abuse—
draws attention to a social problem that was rarely
discussed in Pardo Bazán's day and indeed has only recently become the topic of widespread attention. The following comment, which she made seventeen years after the
publication of "Piña," provides a more explicit condemnation of society's complacency in regard to this social ill:
"The Spanish woman enjoys robust health and a long life,
on the average longer than that of the male; nevertheless,
she suffers from one ailment that he does not. This ailment
is not maternity, which is a physiological function rather
than an illness. The ailment that strikes down so many
Spanish women is the knife, brandished by jealous, brutal
hands . . . A national malady, characteristic of this people"
("La mujer española," Blanco y negro, 5 Jan. 1907: 1).*

*Still, while the author is clearly critical of the physical
abuse of females by males in this story, her stance toward
the victim Piña is less straightforward. When Piña dies at
the end of the story, how are we to interpret the difference
between the responses of the narrator's sons and of the
narrator's daughter?*

15

Piña[1] the Cuban, daughter of the sun and quite accustomed to the ardent caresses of that magnificent and resplendent star, died—no doubt from languishing and from the cold—in the damp climate of the northwest, to which she had been exiled by the vagaries of fate.

We had, indeed, spared no effort to sweeten the poor expatriate's life and make it bearable. When she arrived, quaking and debilitated from the long crossing, we quickly cut out and sewed for her a precious orange velvet dress adorned with gold tassels; with considerably bad grace she allowed us to dress her in this, accustomed as she was to unrestrained nudity in her coconut groves. In the end, like it or not, we fitted her out in her dress, and she started to bounce up and down, perhaps satisfied with the gentle warmth she felt. However, with her bad habit of using the five fingers of her hand instead of fork and knife to eat, in two or three days her pretty dress looked frightful. It had looked so smart on her, however, that we couldn't help making others for her from whatever scraps of cloth we had.

That was the good thing about Piña: from scarcely a yard of fabric we could cut her a proper full-length coat, and from half a muslin pastry cloth an exquisite quilt could be made for her. And she so loved to cuddle up and

---

[1] *Piña* means "pineapple."

pamper herself in her warm little corner, where the very flow of her blood and the breath from her delicate little chest created a sweet space that brought her vague memories of her native clime!

At night she curled up in her little comforter; but by day her vivacious temperament would not allow her to remain in that position, and all day long we saw her jump, grab on to the rope that hung from a small ring in the ceiling, swing to and fro, perform acrobatics, bare her teeth for us, and utter shrill cries. If we took her an acorn, half a carrot, or a grape, she would extend her ice-cold black hand with its agile little fingers, and break the fruit, the sweet, or whatever it was into small pieces; and while she nibbled it and savored it and let it slide, half chewed, into the two pockets under her cheeks that adorned her grimacing face, she watched us benevolently but not without some suspicion through her squinted, gold, childlike eyes, eyes veiled by an indefinable melancholy.

Seeing her a prisoner behind that wire mesh filled us with sorrow. But curse the person who freed such a creature! Half an hour after she was let out, there wouldn't be an unbroken dish in the house. The day she managed to escape our unrelenting vigilance, she did more damage than a cyclone. She knocked over two flowerpots, shattering them to pieces, of course; she tore the pages out of three or four books; she carried the coachman's cap all over the house, finally throwing it into the firebox; she destroyed a hurricane lamp and drank the oil; and she ended up half strangled in the wires of an electric doorbell. By some miracle we got her out alive, her escape making clear to us once again that liberty is not for everyone, that it is only for those who can enjoy it in moderation.

But of course poor Piña, seeing herself free and alone, had thought she was in her tropical groves, where no one raises a fuss over a broken branch here or there. Once the uproar of her first inebriation had passed, Piña fell into a deep depression, I don't know whether in reaction to the feverish activity in which she spent those few hours or because of the effects of the oil lamp. It was sad to view her through the wire, so despondent, so pale, the skin of her throat wrinkled, and her hair standing on end, disheveled. Her immobility made the cage seem an even sadder place, and her plaintive howling had a certain resemblance to the muffled whimper of a sick or weak child. We realized that we had to try some heroic remedy, and so we commissioned a ship captain, the first who would accept the assignment, to find a groom for Piña.

Nothing less than a groom for her!

It is important to know that Piña retained her purity,

innocence, modesty, and all those things that should be kept by young ladies worthy of the public's consideration and respect. The flower—if it can be called that— of her virginity was intact. And though there was no explicit sign that would justify the presumptuous and offensive supposition that Piña was passing through that crucial period in which maidens long for a husband, the despair and depression into which she had sunk were reason enough for us to provide her with the supreme distraction of love and hearth. And so we coughed up five duros, and the husband, very shiny of fur and very quick of movement, entered the cage as if it were conquered territory.

Could it be that that dashing fellow was steeped in the theories of Luis Vives, Fray Luis de León,[2] and other thinkers who consider females to have been created exclusively for the male's greater convenience, to cater to his dignity, his pride and power, and the satisfaction of his whims? Could it have been the fellow's intention to put into practice the ironic commandment of the popu-

---

[2] References are to Juan Luis Vives (1492–1540) and Luis Ponce de León (1527?–1591), humanist scholars of the Counter Reformation. Vives is the author of *Instrucción de la mujer cristiana* (The Instruction of the Christian Woman), which strongly influenced Fray Luis's *La perfecta casada* (The Perfect Wife). Both works advocate restricting women to the domestic sphere and a woman's subservience to the male sex; they have been highly influential in the development of cultural notions of sex roles in Spain.

lar muse, which says, "You must treat your wife as you would a pack mule"?

Or might it be that he fell prey to a spirit of resentment and vengeance when he noticed that the young bride received him with obvious coolness and a marked lack of affection? What I can affirm is that from the first day Piña's husband (to whom we gave the telling name Coco[3]) became a loathsome tyrant. I don't know whether anything like conjugal caresses transpired between them. All I can say is that—either out of an excess of modesty (unusual in people of their race) or because no caresses existed between them—we never saw Coco and Piña treat each other in any way different from that which I will now describe.

While Piña cowered in a corner of her cage amidst vegetable parings, mangled carrots, and crushed pears, her husband would approach her and calmly sit on her back, as if on a comfortable stool, placing his two feet on her haunches and grabbing the poor thing by the throat with both his hands, putting her at risk of strangulation. Coco maintained his balance in this awkward position, and once in a while for entertainment he would give his

---

[3] Coco means not only "coconut" but also "bogeyman." Many Spanish expressions use *coco,* such as *hacer cocos* ("to make a fuss over nothing") and *ser un coco* ("to be very ugly"), all of which come into play here.

victim a cruel bite, an unexpected blow, or a sharp slap over the eyes. Trembling, frightened, curled up into a ball, she remained motionless, because the slightest attempt to escape would cost her innumerable bites and blows. It was incomprehensible that the torturer did not tire of being suspended in this position, but he didn't, sitting erect on his living pedestal like the oriental satraps who lay a rug of human bodies at the foot of their thrones. If we approached the cage, offering the couple some little fruit delicacy or sweet, it was Coco's paw that appeared through the wire grating, and his mouth was the only one into which disappeared the strawberries or almonds presented to the couple. On occasion, overcome by the instinct for sweets, Piña would try to stretch out her hand, and desire would shine in her fading eyes with their wrinkled silken lids; but immediately the husband's teeth would press down upon her ears, a hard slap would fall on her neck, and any spark of gluttony would give way to the pressure of pain and fear.

Fear . . . why? Herein lies the problem that troubled me when I stopped to think about the fate of that mistreated little Cuban. Her husband—or, rather, her tyrant—was of the same stature as she; he was not stronger or more agile than she, not in possession of sharper teeth, or of anything, in short, on which to base his despotism. This was the enigma: What moral influence, what sovereignty does the male sex exercise over the female sex that it can subjugate it so and can reduce it easily, without opposition or resistance, to the role of obedient, resigned passivity, to the acceptance of martyrdom?

During the first days, it would have been impossible to predict the victor in a hand-to-hand fight. Would it be male or female, Piña or Coco? But then the female didn't even try to defend herself: she bowed her head and accepted the yoke. It wasn't love that bent her to submission, for we never saw her master give her anything but yanks of the hair, slaps, and bloody bites. It was simply the prestige of masculinity, the tradition of the absurd obedience of the female, slave since prehistoric times. He wanted to use her as his rug, and she offered her spine. There wasn't even a hint of protest.

And Piña was dying. Every day she was paler, thinner, shakier, more indifferent toward everything. No longer did she scratch herself, make faces, scold us, or climb up the rope. The weak nervous system of this tropical creature was breaking down; the lack of food brought on anemia, and anemia set the stage for consumption. Until then we had played the part of society, which doesn't like to interfere in domestic affairs and allows the husband to finish off his wife if he so desires, since she is, after all, his property. But in the face of this excessive evil, we decided to play Providence and create a separate section in the cage where we confined the executioner, leaving the martyr alone and free.

To tell about Coco's facial expressions and shrill shrieks would make a never-ending story. When he saw that we offered Piña sweets and food, his cries of envy and anger filled the cage. And at first Piña—oh, the habit of fear and resignation!—didn't dare savor the gift, as though the tyrant could impose his will on her even through the bars, even when it was impossible for him to harm her. But as the days passed, Piña's confidence was reborn, just as the hair grew back on the nape of her abraded neck. Her health bloomed again, she put on weight, her agate eyes shone, her teeth seemed whiter, her prehensile tail was full of fun, and her mischievous hands played outside the bars, taking pleasure in delousing, by way of a caress, all who approached her prison. If we add to this the approaching summer, the warm temperature, the sun's frequent visits to the windowed gallery where we kept the cage, one can understand the happiness and rejuvenation of Coco's wife, revealed in the fine state of her fur and in her quick movements and gestures.

Much to Piña's delight, we moved to our country house, and there she was permitted to roam the gardens and to climb trees up to the length of her light chain. She danced atop the acacias and in the foliage of the camellias, perhaps dreaming that the sky was not azure but indigo, that the small orchards were thick mangrove swamps, and that the fish swimming in the ponds were not red carp but brown alligators that left a trail of musk in the water.

And we no longer kept her in the cage. We were happy to tie her chain to a small ring at night. One morning we found the ring and a broken link from the chain, but no Piña. After an extensive search she was found, shivering and half dead, on an eave of the roof. Drunk with liberty and light, she had confused the nights of Galicia with the warm luminous nights of the Antilles, and the dew, fog, and cold of dawn had inflicted on her a mortal wound.

She passed away just like a person or, rather, like a child: coughing, moaning softly, with an agonized death rattle, her eyes glassing over, her tear ducts growing moist. My children insisted on burying her solemnly in the garden. They dug her grave at the base of the great orange tree, not far from the foot of a sage bush all abloom; there they laid down the body, wrapped in a white cloth; they covered it with dirt and over the grave cast flowers, shells, and even colored stamps and Easter prints. While the two older children, the boys, cried out all the tears of their pious little hearts, my little girl, pursing her winsome lips like a trumpet and displaying the gestures and pouts she deemed appropriate for expressing grief, pronounced these words—a condemnation of sentimentality and an indication of a jovial and antiromantic character:

"I, too, wanted to cry for Piña. But I can't!"

THE OLDEST STORY

"The Oldest Story" most clearly anticipates contemporary feminist commentary in its suggestion of the modern-day joke that "Adam was a rough draft." The story of Genesis, which has often been seen as a justification—or reflection— of misogyny, is rewritten. Eve's role in the commission of the "original sin" is effaced; instead, she is presented as a slightly superior companion to Adam. The thematic emphasis is on the origin of misogyny rather than of sin. In refusing to blame Eve for humankind's downfall, Pardo Bazán echoes her literary hero Benito Jerónimo Feijóo, who pointed out the fallacy of this misogynistic belief in his "Defensa de las mujeres" ("Defense of Women"), a long essay included in his Teatro crítico universal *(1726-40). But, as Lou Charnon-Deutsch notes, "Cuento primitivo" can also be read as a response to the misogynistic "Cuento futuro" (A Story of the Future) by Pardo Bazán's critic Clarín, published a year earlier (* Narratives of Desire: Nineteenth-Century Spanish Fiction by Women *[University Park: Pennsylvania State UP, 1994] 204).*

In her story, Pardo Bazán suggests a notion she elaborates in several other works: that woman's victimization is partially caused by her being brainwashed at the hands of the patriarchal culture. Having been told so often that she is inferior, a woman begins to believe it. Pardo Bazán thus challenges the prevailing discourse that posits feminine submission as biologically—and divinely—ordained.

> *Equally of interest is the way she encodes her revision of Genesis. It is told not by the narrator but by the narrator's acquaintance, who is elaborately characterized as eccentric, obsessive, heterodoxical, and perhaps a bit crazy. This idiosyncratic version of the Adam and Eve story, then, can hardly be attributed to Pardo Bazán herself.*

I once had an old friend, a man with a sense of humor and a bit of the March Hare or, as a classical author would say, someone crazed by his own caprice. He suffered from an illness that was quite the fashion fifty years ago but now is passé: a systematic loathing for everything having to do with religion, church, faith, and the clergy—a loathing that manifested itself in jokes that were rather Voltairean, little stories as spicy as chili peppers, materialist arguments that were so innocent they were childlike, and crude sexual theories. All these were quite different from his true feelings and actions, since, despite his display of vulgar impiety, he was always a man of pure habits, kind heart, and consummate honesty.

One of the things that gave my friend the opportunity to rant was exegesis, meaning the interpretation—scathing, of course—of the sacred books. He was always going on and on about the Bible and arguing with Father Scío of San Miguel. He insisted that the priest should have been named not Father Scío but Father

Nescío,[1] saying that it would be necessary to don spectacles to be able to see his learning and that the priest stumbled over himself continually within the murky mazes of those labyrinthine and nebulous texts which were as obscure as they were ancient. My friend, without realizing that he was in the same position as Father Scío—indeed worse, for he lacked the theological and philological learning of that venerable biblical scholar—gamely "corrected" the priest's arguments, uttering odd absurdities that, taken in jest, helped us pass the long winter evenings in the village, when the rain soaks the earth and drips off the bare branches of the trees and the dogs howl fearfully, announcing imaginary perils.

On a night like this, after having gulped down the light milk punch we used to drink to ward off the cold, and with the card game in full force, my friend lit into the Book of Genesis and recast—in his own way—the story of Creation. Let nobody think that he revised it in the Darwinian sense; that would be too close to the Old Testament story of the Six Days, in which the creation of the universe ascends from the inorganic to the organic, from lower organisms to higher ones. No: Cre-

---

[1] Felipe Scío de San Miguel (1738-96) was known for his biblical scholarship and for his translation of the Bible. *Scio* is Latin for "I know"; *nescio* means "I do not know, I am ignorant." The Spanish word *necio* means someone stubborn or foolish, an ignoramus.

ation, according to my friend—who was so well-informed that no doubt he had conversed with the Creator Himself—took the form you will discover if you continue reading. All I am doing is transcribing the essence of the account—though I do not promise that the style is exactly right.

"On the first day God created man. Yes, man; Adam, made from the mud or clay of the amorphous planet. Now, do you think God experimented and tested and fumbled about, taking a week of practice, in order to end up with such a funny-looking creature as man? Certainly not. The only thing that explains and excuses man is that he sprang forth from the spark of improvisation, created when the Lord, on the spur of the moment, decided to condense the chaotic matter of space into spherical form.

"And He hatched man first, for a very simple reason: planning, as He did, that Adam would be lord and master of all creation, God thought it proper to give him a say in the constitution of His kingdoms and domains. In sum, God, in the role of a good father, wanted to make His creature happy by allowing him to speak up and state his preferences with his own big mouth.

"As Adam stirred, still aching from the pinches of the divine fingers that molded his form, he looked around: and as darkness still covered the face of the abyss, he felt sadness and fear, and he wanted to see, to take pleasure in the resplendent light. God pronounced the well-known *Fiat lux,* and the glorious sun appeared in the firmament. Man saw, and his soul overflowed with joy.

"However, he soon noticed that what he saw was neither particularly varied nor very entertaining—an immense and barren expanse, sterile land on which the burning light of the sun flickered and rebounded like flaming arrows. Adam moaned softly, muttering that he was roasting and that the earth seemed like a wasteland to him. And without delay, God raised up vegetation, the soft velvety grass that covers the ground, the flowering shrubs that decorate and embellish it, and the majestic trees that cast their delightful shadows over it. When Adam observed that this enchanting mantle over the earth's surface was beginning to wilt, vast oceans appeared, along with rushing rivers, laughing fountains, and dew that fell in pearl droplets on the fields. And when Adam complained that so much sun was bothering his eyes, our tireless God, instead of giving His handiwork tinted goggles, created nothing less than the moon and the stars and established the tranquil cycle of night and day.

"With all this, the first man was beginning to find Eden livable. He knew how to protect himself from the heat and how to shelter himself from the cold. God had satisfied his hunger and quenched his thirst right away, offering him delectable fruits and pure springs. Adam was able to wander freely in the thickets, the jungles, the valleys, the idyllic gardens, and the grottos of his privileged mansion. He was allowed to gather all the flowers, taste all the varied and sweet species of fruit, enjoy all the waters, lie down in all the soft beds of grass, and live without care or desire, letting the days of his eternal youth slip by in a world that was always young. Nonetheless, this idyllic good fortune was not enough for Adam: he missed having company, other living beings who would liven the confines of Paradise.

"And God, ever accommodating, hurried to surround Adam with a variety of animals. Some were graceful, gentle, handsome, and tame—like the pigeon and the turtledove; others friendly, playful, and mischievous—like the monkey and the cat. Still others were loyal and faithful, like the dog; and still others, like the lion, were beautiful and terrible in appearance—although for Adam they were all humble and tame, and he even had the tigers eating out of his hand. Since God wanted to make sure that Adam would never again feel lonely for want of other living beings to keep him company, He created animals by the millions and multiplied organisms, from the tiniest infusoria suspended in the air and water to the monstrous megatheres hiding deep in the jungles. He wanted Adam to find life everywhere, energetic, self-renewing, and full of passion: life that thrives in every clime and needs only the slightest spark of fire for its flame to be kindled.

"At first Adam was amused by these ragamuffins and played happily with them as if he were a child. Nonetheless, after a time, he realized that he was wearying of the inferior beings, just as he had wearied of the sun, the moon, the oceans, and the plants. As the sun rises and sets in an identical manner every day, so do creatures repeat the same antics, the same actions and movements—all predictable beforehand, depending on the species. The monkey will always imitate and grimace; the colt will leap and be graceful; the dog will be vigilant and devoted; the nightingale won't dream of changing his sonatas; as for the cat, that sluggard spends hours on end just purring, as we all know. And so Adam woke up one morning, thinking life was stupid and Paradise insipid.

"God is a quick study, and so He immediately realized that Adam was bored. He brought him to task, severely rebuking him. What did his lordship want? Didn't he have everything he could possibly desire? Didn't he enjoy supreme peace and enviable happiness in Eden? Didn't all creation obey him? Wasn't he now a very important person?

"Adam confessed with noble frankness that it was precisely that calm, that security that had him at his wit's end. He longed for something unexpected, for some kind of excitement, even if it cost him his peace and soporific serenity.

"And so God, regarding him with pity, came near him and subtly removed—not a rib, as most people would have it—but bits of his brain, a few smidgens of his heart, some nerve bundles, some fragments of bone, a few ounces of blood—in a word, a little bit of each part of him. And since God—having a choice—was not going to choose the worst parts, He of course took the very best bits, the most delicate and select bits—the very flower of the male, so to speak, from which to mold and create the female. So when Eve was finally created, Adam ended up less than he had been before, and, we must say, rather the worse for wear.

"For His part, God, knowing that He had in His hands the most exquisite essence of man, took great pains to mold it lovingly and give it shape. He didn't dare squeeze His fingers as tightly as when He had fashioned man. From His soft and enchanting caresses came those soft curves, those shapely and elegant contours that are such a contrast to the roughness and rigidity of the masculine form.

"When Eve was just right, God took her by the hand and presented her to Adam. Adam was enthralled and astounded by her and thought he must be in the presence of a celestial being, a luminous cherub. And for some days he continued to think this, never tiring of looking at her again and again, of admiring and flattering and buttering up the precious creature. It was in vain that Eve protested that she was made of the same clay as he; Adam didn't believe it. He swore that she came from another region, from the blue spaces where the stars spin, from the pure ether that holds the sun's orb, or perhaps from the ocean of light where spirits float before the throne of the Almighty. It is thought that it was about this time that Adam composed the first sonnet ever.

"This state of affairs lasted until Adam, without the need of any insinuations from the treacherous serpent, got an overwhelming craving for an apple that Eve guarded with great care. I know for a fact that Eve guarded it and that she didn't give it up so easily. This passage of the Scriptures is one of the most distorted. In the end, despite Eve's defense, Adam won out, since he was the stronger, and he wolfed down the apple. No sooner had the poorly chewed pieces of the fruit of perdition landed in his stomach than—oh wondrous change! incredible reversal!—instead of taking Eve for a seraph, he took her for a demon or a wild beast. Instead of thinking her pure and without blemish, he thought her a repository of all iniquity and evil. Instead of attributing to her his happiness and his ecstasy, he blamed her for his restlessness, for his sorrows, even for the banish-

ment God imposed on them and for their eternal wan-
derings down that thorny, thistle-filled path.

"The fact is, by dint of hearing this so much, Eve came
to believe it too. She acknowledged her blame, her memory of her origin escaped her, and she no longer dared
claim that she was of the same substance as man—not
better, not worse, but just a little more refined. And the
myth of the Book of Genesis is repeated in the life of
each and every Eve: before the apple, Adam erects an
altar to her and worships her on it. After the apple, he
removes her from the altar, and then it's off to the stable
with her, or to the dump . . .

"Nevertheless," my friend would add by way of a moral—after downing another glass of the mild punch—
"since Eve was formed from Adam's most intimate
essence, Adam, though heaping calumny on her, all the
while goes after her like the rope after the bucket. He
doesn't stop running after her until he has no breath left
in his body and the roof of his mouth is cold. In truth,
his wish has been granted: ever since God brought Eve
to him, man has never been bored again, nor has he ever
again enjoyed the peace and quiet of Eden. Banished
from such a pleasant mansion, he can only catch a
glimpse of it—for an instant—in the depths of Eve's
eyes, where a reflection of its image remains."

MY SUICIDE

Pardo Bazán dedicated "My Suicide" to the post-Romantic poet Ramón de Campoamor (1817-1901). In the preface to Cuentos de amor *(Love Stories) (6-7), she explains that it was Campoamor who first suggested the story to her. But the connection with Campoamor does not end there; the style of this story duplicates, in a way that could be read as parody, the poet's "oscillation between impersonal observation and cloying sentimentality" (D. L.* Shaw, A Literary History of Spain: The Nineteenth Century *[New York: Barnes, 1972] 66). The same oscillation is reflected in the shifts in point of view between the deluded narrator-protagonist and the disenchanted narrator. As in "Sister Aparición," Pardo Bazán engages in an oblique attack on Romanticism's and post-Romanticism's emblemizing of woman as embodiment of sin and object of desire.*

With her dead, motionless, laid out in that horrible coffin of varnished mahogany I could still picture before me, with its malevolently lustrous gold moldings, what was left for me in this world? I had concentrated all my light, my joy, my dreams in her, all my pleasure . . . and for her to disappear like that, suddenly, snatched away in the flower of her youth and seductive beauty, was no less than to summon me in a melodious voice—a magical voice, the voice that resonated inside me, producing divine harmony: "Since you love me, come follow me."

To follow her! Yes, that was the only ambition worthy of my affection and commensurate with my pain, and it was the cure for the eternal abandonment to which the adorable creature had condemned me by fleeing to far-off regions.

To follow her, rejoin her, surprise her on the other side of the funereal river, and clasp her to me deliriously, exclaiming, "Here I am. Did you think I could live without you? See how I learned to seek and find you so that from today on no power on earth or in heaven can separate us."

Determined, I resolved to realize my goal in the very sanctum where so many hours of happiness had slipped by unnoticed in cadence with the gentle beating of our hearts . . . As I entered, I forgot my misfortune, and it appeared to me that *she*, alive and beaming, came forward to greet me as before, raising the curtain to see me the sooner, her eyes radiating her welcome, her cheeks flushed with happiness. Over there was the wide sofa where we used to sit pressed so closely together that it could just as well have been oh so narrow. Over there was the fireplace where she would stretch out her little feet toward the flame as I jealously vied to warm them with my hands, into which they fit so comfortably. Over there was the armchair where she retreated during brief moments of childish vexation to double the reward of reconciliation. Over there stood the iridescent crystal vase by Salviatti, with the last flowers—now dry and pale—that her hand had artistically arranged to celebrate my presence. And over there, finally, as if in marvelous resurrection of the past, immortalizing her adorable figure, was she, she herself . . . that is, her portrait, that great painting, life-size, a renowned artist's masterpiece that represented her seated, adorned in one of my favorite raiments, a simple and graceful white silk sheath that enveloped her in a cloud of chiffon. It was her familiar attitude, her fascinating luminous green eyes; it was her mouth, half open as if to exclaim, in a mixture of flattery and rebuke, the affectionately impatient "How late you are!"; it was her curved arms, which used to encircle my neck as the wave surrounds the waist of the drowning castaway. In sum, it was a most faithful rendering of the features and tones through which a soul had captivated me, an enchanting image that for me signified the best of existence. There, before all that spoke worlds to me of her and reminded me of our bond, right there at the foot of the beloved portrait, kneeling on the sofa, I would squeeze the trigger of the double-barreled English pistol that held in its bosom the cure for all misfortune and the passage to the port where *she* awaited me. In this way her image would not fade from my eyes, not even for one second; I would close them gazing on her and I would open them again to see her, not in oil but in spirit.

Dusk was falling, and because I wanted to contemplate the portrait to my heart's content while resting the pistol barrel on my temple, I ignited the lamp and all the candles in the candelabras. There was a candelabra with three arms on the *secrétaire* of inlaid rosewood, and as I brought the match to one of the candlewicks, it occurred to me that my letters would be there, along with my portrait— memories of our enduring and intimate story. A vigorous desire to reread those pages impelled me to open the desk.

It should be pointed out that I possessed no letters from her: I had returned them all after reading them, out of caution, out of respect, and out of gentlemanly decency. I thought that she might not have had the heart to destroy them and that from the niches of the *secrétaire* her insinuating, beloved voice would rise again, repeating the sweet phrases that had not had time to engrave themselves in my memory. I did not hesitate—does a man who is going to die hesitate?—before forcing the lock of that exquisite little piece of furniture. The cover splintered apart, and I reached feverishly into the small drawers, anxiously rummaging through them.

Only one contained letters. The others were filled with ribbons, jewels, trinkets, fans, and perfumed handkerchiefs. Slowly I took hold of the packet, which was bound with a luxurious piece of silk brocade, and stroked it as one strokes the head of a loved one before planting a kiss there, and, walking toward the light, I prepared to read. It was her handwriting: these were her beloved letters. My heart sang in gratitude that the departed had shown this delicate refinement in keeping them there as testimonial to her passion, as a codicil in which she bequeathed to me her tenderness.

I untied, I unfolded, and I began to decipher. At first, I thought I recognized the ardent phrases, the passionate protestations, and even the allusions to intimate details that can be known only to two souls. Nevertheless, on the second page an indefinable uneasiness, a vague terror, passed through my imagination, as a bullet passes through the air before it wounds. I rejected the idea, I cursed it, but it came back, back . . . back, reinforced by the paragraphs on the third page, which were swarming with hints and little details that could not have referred to me and the story of my love. By the fourth page, no shadow of doubt remained: the letter had been written to another and recalled different days, different hours, different events, all unknown to me.

I read the rest of the packet; I went through each letter

one by one, as a stubborn hope urged me to clutch at straws. Perhaps the remaining letters were mine, and just that one letter had slipped into this group, as an isolated memento of a bygone love, long since relegated to oblivion. But, as I examined the pages, as I read—rubbing my eyes—a paragraph here, another there, I had to admit it: none of the letters in the packet had been addressed to me. The letters I had received and religiously returned were probably to be found amongst the ashes in the fireplace. And the ones *she* had preserved forever like treasures, in a hidden corner of the *secrétaire,* in the room that had been witness to our happiness, indicated as precisely as a compass points toward north the true orientation of the heart I had thought was mine. But there was more pain, more infamy yet! From those terrible lines, from those pages written in a hand I would have recognized from all others in the world, it dawned on me that *perhaps . . . at the same time . . .* or *very shortly before . . .* And a voice shouted ironically in my ear, "Now! . . . Now you really ought to take your life, you wretch!"

Tears of rage scalded my eyes; I positioned myself, as I had resolved, before the portrait, gripped the pistol, lifted the double barrel . . . and, aiming coolly, without haste, with a steady hand . . . fired two shots and shot through the two green, luminous eyes that had fascinated me so.

41

SISTER APARICIÓN

"Sister Aparición" is a particularly rich text, inviting commentary on a wide variety of issues that range from the cultural processes of literary canon formation to the confirmation of male subjectivity through sexual conquest. The narrative structure plays very subtly with the question of "masculine" and "feminine" perspective: only at the end of the story, in the gender of the adjective admirada *("surprised"), do we discover that the speaker is female.*

In her preface to Cuentos de amor, *the author mentions that this story is based on a real-life joke played by one of the nation's greatest Romantic poets. The story is thick with clues that identify the poet as José de Espronceda. For example, the village of A*** could refer to Almendralejo, where the poet was baptized; the reference to Badajoz as the provincial capital makes this almost certain. The fictional Camargo's work* Accursed Archangel *suggests one of Espronceda's most famous poems,* El diablo mundo *(This Devilish World), and evokes a common Esproncedian image for woman, that of the fallen angel. Another celebrated poem by Espronceda,* El estudiante de Salamanca *(The Student of Salamanca), is cleverly echoed in the fact that when Camargo first notices Irene, he has returned from his studies in Salamanca. But the most obvious indication that Camargo is Espronceda is the similarity in their public personae, for Espronceda, like Camargo, was at least as*

42

famous for his prolific sexual adventures and his subversive political activities as he was for his poetry.

Pardo Bazán's remarks on her story lend particular insight not only to the interpretation of the story but also to the relation between realism and reality, to the author's relationship with her public, and to the critical dispositions of her contemporaries: "Many people were shocked by 'Sister Aparición.' I read the story over again, slowly, and I cannot understand what provokes such horror, except the cruel reality which throbs throughout it. . . . I imposed on [Irene] enough years of mortification and weeping to placate even the most easily shocked. The truth is that I do not know what ever happened to the victim of that infamous prank played by one of our greatest Romantic poets" (10–11).

Aparición commonly means "vision," as in a miraculous vision of the Virgin. But it also translates as "apparition" or "ghost." The name reinforces the importance of the gaze in this story.

In the convent of the Poor Clares at S***, I saw, through the low double grille, a nun prostrate in adoration. She was turned toward the main altar and lay absolutely still, her face pressed against the floor and her arms outstretched in the shape of a cross. She seemed no more alive than the recumbent forms of the queen and the infanta whose alabaster crypts adorned the choir. Suddenly the nun rose, no doubt to breathe, and I was able to make out her features. I saw that she had been very beautiful in her youth, just as one can discern once-splendid palaces by the ruins of their walls. The nun could have been eighty just as easily as ninety. Her sepulchral yellow face, her trembling head, her ravaged mouth, her white eyebrows—all revealed an age so advanced that it was insensitive to the passing of time.

The outstanding feature of that ghostly face, which already belonged to the other world, were the eyes. Strangely, in defiance of age, they conserved their fire, their intense blackness, their fiercely passionate and dramatic expression. A glance from those eyes could never be forgotten. Such volcanic eyes would have been inexplicable in a nun who had entered the cloister offering God an innocent heart; they betrayed a tumultuous past; they radiated the sinister light of some terrible memory. And although I felt a burning curiosity, I did not expect Providence to furnish me with anyone who knew the nun's secret.

Chance nonetheless fulfilled my wishes. That very night, at the round table of the inn, I struck up a conversation with an elderly gentleman, who was very talkative and more than moderately perceptive, the sort that enjoys filling in visitors from out of town. Flattered by my interest, he opened wide the archive of his sharp memory. As soon as I mentioned the convent of the Clares and told him about the singular impression the nun's gaze had made on me, my guide exclaimed:

"Ah! Sister Aparición! Of course, of course . . . There is something inexplicable in those eyes. Her history is written there. Let me tell you, the two furrows in her cheeks, which up close look like canals, have been cut by tears. She has wept for more than forty years. After so many days, water runs salty. But the fact is that the water has not extinguished the fire in her eyes . . . Poor Sister Aparición! I can tell you the story of her life better than anybody, for my father met her when she was young and I think even wooed her a bit. She was a goddess, you see!

"Her secular name was Irene. Her parents were of the gentry—small-town rich folk; they had several other off-spring, but they lost them, so they concentrated on Irene all the love and indulgence given an only child. The town where she was born is called A***. And destiny, which weaves with our very crib sheets the rope that eventually hangs us, disposed that in that same town a famous poet would be born, a few years before Irene."

Getting ahead of the narrator, I let out a cry and pro-nounced the name of the glorious author of *Accursed Archangel,* perhaps the finest exemplar of the Romantic fever. It was a name that carried in its syllables an echo of disdainful arrogance, mocking contempt, bitter irony, and desperate and blasphemous nostalgia. That name and the nun's eyes became blurred in my imagination, and when I put them together, though one did not give me the key to the other, they suggested a drama of the heart—the kind of drama that gushes blood.

"The same," my interlocutor replied, "the illustrious Juan de Camargo, pride of the little town of A***, which has no mineral baths, no miraculous saint, no cathedral, no Roman gravestones, or anything notable to show those who visit there but which proudly repeats, 'Camargo was born in this house on the plaza . . .'"

"I see," I interrupted. "Now I understand. Sister Aparición . . . I mean, Irene, fell in love with Camargo, he scorned her, and in order to forget, she entered the convent . . ."

"Ha!" exclaimed the narrator, smiling. "Wait, wait a minute. If it were only that! One sees that kind of thing every day; it wouldn't even be worth telling. In Sister Aparición's case, there's more than meets the eye. Be patient, we'll get there yet.

"As a child, Irene had seen Juan Camargo a thousand times without ever speaking to him, because he was already a young man, unsociable and aloof, who didn't even associate with the other young men in town. When Irene emerged from her cocoon, Camargo, an orphan, was already studying law in Salamanca and came to his guardian's house only during holidays. One summer, on entering A***, the student happened to raise his eyes to Irene's window and he noticed the girl, whose eyes were fixed on him . . . eyes that said, 'Surrender,' eyes like two black suns. You have seen for yourself what those eyes still are today. Camargo reined in his hack so as to delight in that unsurpassed beauty, for Irene was stunningly beautiful. But, as red as a poppy, the girl drew away from the window and slammed it shut. That very night Camargo, who was already beginning to have his poetry published in the local newspapers, wrote some splendid verses describing the effect the sight of Irene had on him as he entered his home town . . . He wrapped a stone with the verses and at nightfall flung it at her window. The window shattered, the young girl picked up the paper and read the verses, not once but a hundred times, a thousand times, drinking them in, soaking them up. Yet those verses, which do not appear in Camargo's collected poetry, were a declaration not of love but of something strange—a mixture of complaint and curse. The poet lamented that the purity and beauty of the girl at the window had not been made for him, a reprobate. If he were to come close, that white lily would wilt . . . Following this episode with the verses, Camargo gave no sign of remembering Irene's existence in the world, and in October he left for Madrid. The restless period of his life began, a period of political adventure and literary activity.

"After Camargo's departure, Irene became sad and then ill and dispirited. Her parents tried to distract her. They took her to Badajoz for a while, introduced her to

47

young men, took her to dances. She had her admirers, her flatterers; but neither her mood nor her health improved.

"She could think of nothing but Camargo, to whom was applicable all that Byron said of Lara[1]—that those who saw him did not forget him, that the memory of him always came to mind, since such men defy disdain and oblivion. Irene herself did not think she was in love; she simply considered herself the victim of a curse that sprang from those somber, strange verses. The fact is that Irene had what is now called an obsession, and Camargo 'appeared' to her at all hours—pale, serious, his curly hair clouding his pensive brow. Irene's parents, seeing that their daughter was wasting away from a mysterious ailment, decided to take her to the capital, where there are not only great doctors to consult but also great diversions.

"When Irene arrived in Madrid, Camargo was famous. His fiery, haughty verses, expressing a strong and nervous sentiment, set the new style; his adventures and peculiarities of character were food for gossip. He kept company with a gang of scoundrels, clever, nonchalant bohemians, who nightly invented new deviltries, from disturbing the sleep of honest citizens to performing or-

[1] Lara, the eponymous protagonist of Byron's poem, is a misanthrope.

giastic feats referred to in certain blasphemous, obscene poems, which some critics insist are not really Camargo's. The gang alternated drinking bouts and licentiousness with sessions in Masonic lodges and political committees. Camargo was already paving the way for his exile. Irene's ingenuous and provincial family knew of none of this, and when they came upon the poet in the street, they greeted him cheerfully; after all, he was from 'back home.'

"Once again Camargo was surprised by the young woman's beauty, and when he noticed that the lovely child's pale cheeks reddened as she looked at him, he decided to accompany the family and later promised he would pay a visit. The simple village people were flattered, and their satisfaction grew when they saw, several days after Camargo had kept his promise, that Irene was reviving. Unaware of his reputation, they considered Camargo a possible son-in-law and agreed to frequent visits.

"I can see by your expression that you think you know where this is going. You do not! Irene, spellbound, mad, as though she had drunk a potion of herbs, nonetheless went six months before she consented to meeting him alone, in his own house. The girl's honest resistance led Camargo's cronies to mock him; and pride, which is the poisonous root of certain romanticisms such as Byron's and Camargo's, inspired him to make a bet, to take satanic, infernal revenge. He requested, implored, left, returned, made her jealous, feigned plans of suicide, and tried so many tactics that Irene, overwhelmed by all this, at last consented to the dangerous meeting. Thanks to a miracle of bravery and propriety, she left it pure and unstained—and Camargo suffered a ridicule that drove him mad with spite.

"At the second meeting, Irene's resistance crumbled; her mind was clouded and she was vanquished. And when she lay in the scoundrel's arms, trembling and confused, her eyelids closed, he burst into loud guffaws and drew back the curtains—and Irene saw herself being devoured by the impure eyes of eight or ten young men, who also laughed and applauded with sarcasm.

"Irene bolted to her feet and, without covering herself, shoulders bare and hair flying, lurched down the stairs and out into the street. She arrived home followed by a crowd of street urchins who flung mud and rocks at her. She never told anyone where she had been or what had happened. My father found out because he happened to be a friend of one of those involved in Camargo's bet. Irene suffered a seven-day fever from which it seemed she would not recover. As soon as she did recover, she entered this convent, as far as possible from A***. Her penance has astounded the nuns: incredible fasts, bread mixed with ashes, three days without drink, winter nights spent barefoot and on her knees in prayer—and she wears an iron collar around her neck, a crown of thorns under her wimple, and a rasp at her waist.

"What most impressed the other nuns, who consider her a saint, was her constant weeping. They say—but it must be nothing but a tale—that once she filled her drinking bowl with her tears. And, if you can believe this, let me tell you that her eyes were suddenly left without a tear and aglow as you have observed! This happened more than twenty years ago; and pious souls believe it was a sign of God's pardon. Nonetheless, Sister Aparición no doubt does not consider herself forgiven, because, old and shrunken like a mummy, she continues to fast and pray and to wear a hair shirt."

"She must be doing penance for two," I said, surprised[2] that my chronicler's insight failed him on this point. "Do you think that Sister Aparición does not remember the poor soul of Camargo?"

---

[2] In Spanish, the feminine adjective indicates, for the first time in the text, that the narrator is a woman.

MEMENTO

"Memento" deals with a topic that is still largely considered taboo in contemporary Western culture: sexual desire in older women. The shocking effect of the story is softened by the use of a male narrator who expresses the repugnance Pardo Bazán may have expected her readers to feel. As in the earlier "First Love," the male speaker shows an asexualization of and disgust toward the aging female body. Pardo Bazán's decision to employ a male narrator renders her treatment of the older woman ambivalent, raising many questions about the author's position. His name, Gabriel, allies him with Gabriel Pardo de la Lage, a character who appears frequently in Pardo Bazán's fiction, not only in her short stories but also in the novels Los pazos de Ulloa, La Madre Naturaleza, *and* Insolación. *In these texts as well, the question of the relation between the character's and the author's beliefs is complex.*

"The most vivid memory of my student days," said the doctor, smiling at the recollection, "is not about my numerous flings and adventures—they were no different from anybody else's—nor is it about certain pretty cheeks whose blushes sweetened my dreams. What I can't forget, what stands out more and more with the passing years, are the socials at the home of my gray-

52

haired aunt Gabriela, who sat every afternoon accompanied by three equally moth-eaten ladies who shared her company, all of them aspiring to have the palm frond on their coffin[1] . . .

"As I have said, the four got together in the afternoon—at night they were too inhibited by fears, aches and pains, and the recitation of their prayers. They met in a small study whose window looked out onto the rich Gothic mullioned windows and the towering walls of the cathedral, and I used to cut short my stroll, just at an hour that teemed with flirtatious young ladies eager for compliments, so that I could lock myself inside those four walls papered in a flowery design that had long ago faded from green to off-white. I would sit in the wide, yielding armchair with its worn springs—it, too, was old—waiting for a light tap on the shoulder from the tiny withered hand covered by the meshwork of a black mitten, while a raspy voice whispered, 'Hello, you here already, you rascal? Candidita[2] will be tickled to death today.'

"Of all the old maids, Cándida was the youngest, since she wasn't quite sixty-three. According to chronicles of those long-ago days when Candidita was in her prime, she had never stood out as a beauty. Her left eye always

---

[1] The palm frond was traditionally placed on the coffins of virgins.
[2] The diminutive *-ita* here holds childlike or affectionate connotations.

drooped somewhat and her back was too hunched. What was pleasing about her was her angelic disposition. Candidita possessed, in keeping with her Christian name, a high degree of gullibility and trust. Whatever unbelievable nonsense I felt like making up, Candidita would swallow effortlessly; yet no one could convince her that any real dishonesty had occurred. Her soul repulsed any talk of evil as her body would reject a foreign object impossible to digest. I had great fun arguing with Candidita when she refused to believe that notorious crimes had happened . . . and as I did so, a feeling of tenderness grew in my heart, a mysterious respect for such an innocent person, who would assuredly rise to heaven when the moment came, unexpectedly, without even removing her black woolen dress and her pigskin shoes.

"My aunt Gabriela, on the other hand, was shrewd and sharp as a tack. Her secluded life in a sleepy provincial city kept her from becoming fully acquainted with the world, and perhaps she exaggerated the low tricks and intrigues that took place within it, but she was always close to the mark and judged with deadly accuracy a thousand times. Proud of her lineage, titled but not a woman of means, she was both an imposing and a modest lady, old-fashioned, her soul more upright than a spear. The other three old maids seemed more her ladies-in-waiting than her friends.

"Doña Aparición was the curiosity of that archaeolog-
ical museum. Beautiful and worldly in her youth, at sev-
enty-six she still showed flashes of coquettishness and
fancies for fashion that made my aunt Gabriela, so majestic in her plain Carmelite dress, purse her lips. Doña
Aparición's wig, with its angelic blond curls and ringlets,
her tight shoes, her light-colored gloves with their eight
buttons, her green-and-pink striped silk dresses, her blue
gossamer fans, and the cluster of artificial flowers pinned
gracefully on her mantilla gave us plenty to laugh about.

"Since she was half blind and almost deaf, her servant
dressed her; sometimes she had her wig on backwards,
or rouge on her nose rather than on her cheeks, or one
lilac glove and one straw-colored glove; and as she suffered from gout, the torturing grip of tight little boots
ended up aggravating her so much that my aunt would
lend her some loose-fitting slippers. Whenever this occurred, Doña Aparición would exclaim without fail:

"'My heavens! Nothing like this has ever happened to
me before. It was a fold in my stocking rubbing against
my heel . . . What a bother to have such delicate skin.'

"Doña Peregrina, the fourth old maid, wouldn't
inflict such punishment on herself just to show off small
feet. Quite to the contrary: she declared herself *sans
façon*. Reduced to a penurious pension, she bought her
drab fly-wing-colored shawls in secondhand shops.

Apart from that, she was a woman of drive and spirit, tall, heavy, with a kind of fusty freshness, if I may express it that way; she was bright-eyed and flushed easily, had a turn for jokes, was at times sanctimonious, but always stayed within the bounds of good humor and decorum.

"How those four ladies doted on me! There are places we go not for our own pleasure but for the pleasure we give others. It had been perhaps ten years since the old maids had seen a young face up close. My solicitous attendance was gallantry of incalculable value that flattered the inextinguishable sentimental vanity of women. If a young man wants to earn a good name, let him be kind to old ladies, to the scorned, to those who have been excluded from the game. Young women show no gratitude for anything. Those four feeble old ladies, with their mild chatter, forged a fabulous reputation for me: so discreet, handsome, charming, studious. They did much to clear my way to a magnificent position and a brilliant marriage. During my exams, I could answer rightly or wrongly, for my grade was assured: such was the secret influence worked on my professors by my spinsters. They never stopped fretting over my health: 'You're so pale, Gabriel . . . What's wrong with you? Watch out for those Jezebels!' And they sent me home remedies, snacks, wine cordials, miracle-working relics, and even bedsheets in case those at the inn 'couldn't be trusted' or 'weren't nicely washed.'

"Then—to liven our gatherings—it occurred to me I might read romantic novels and poetry aloud. No reader has ever had such an appreciative audience. One could say they even held their breath to listen. As I read, their interest, comic in its ingenuousness, grew ever more intense: indignation with the traitors, vivid terror when the good were about to be ambushed by the bad, and a childish joy when virtue triumphed . . . Their exclamations interrupted me: 'That cad is drinking the poison by mistake? A punishment from God!' 'Oh, if Gontrán goes into the woods, he'll run into the other fellow with a dagger! Don't let him go in, don't let him go in!' 'My heavens, he finally stabbed him!' 'Scoundrel!' 'Did you see that the child kidnapped by the puppeteer was the son of a princess?' etcetera. During intense episodes, when lovers exchanged sweet nothings in the moonlight, the old maids went to pieces. A faint blush colored their yellow cheeks; their arid eyes became moist; their shrunken breasts heaved with yearning; the glorious ghost of long-lost youth reappeared, as for a moment a warm and gentle aura lifted those resigned spirits, just as breezes of spring stir the dust in a dry and sterile land.

"The time came for me to leave for the capital to begin my doctoral studies. I broke the news to my old maids and, though it couldn't have been a surprise for them, the effect was nonetheless powerful. My aunt Gabriela, without losing the measure of her dignity, began to tremble. She warned me, in language that showed genuine tenderness, that one should excuse old people if they were upset by good-byes, because they couldn't be sure they would ever again see those who were leaving. Doña Peregrina waved her hands, protested, snorted with rage, insulted me, and finally burst into a flood of tears. Doña Aparición sighed, raised her eyes towards heaven and said, grimacing: 'A young man with such gifts . . . will naturally distinguish himself in the capital! Tomorrow you will receive an emerald pin . . . that belonged to my father.' For her part, Candidita was silent, and a moment later rose, saying she had an urgent visit to make. I took advantage of this to cut the ceremonies short; I exited with her, helped her with her coat, and offered my arm for the walk down the worm-eaten stairs.

"On the first landing, I heard a muffled sob; frail arms encircled my neck, and a face as cold as snow pressed itself to my beard. Suddenly I understood . . . and, believe me, I could not have been more disturbed and more moved had I seen my own mother on her knees before me! Candidita's weight felt like that of a corpse. Thinking she had fainted, I eased her to the balustrade, stammering, full of pity: 'Good-bye, good-bye, you know you are loved.' But, as she would not let me go and I felt like a fool, I pushed her away . . . Doing this made me feel as if I were slitting the throat of a sickly little lamb, and pity forced me to come back and return Candidita's embrace with a rapid and violent caress, amorous in appearance but filial and saintly in intention. And then I ran off, resolving when I made it to the street never again to return to the afternoon socials. That was it! Charity has its limits.

"And now that I too am old, I often think of Candidita. Poor woman!"

Torn Lace

"Torn Lace" is one of several stories in which Pardo Bazán explores the notion that a seemingly insignificant action or even a small gesture can provide us with sudden insight into a person's character. A generation after Pardo Bazán, modernist short story writers would extensively employ epiphany as an important structuring device in terms of both plot and theme. Here, an epiphany leads the protagonist to break off her engagement at the last possible moment. Such elements as the choice of the image of torn lace for the story's title and the presentation of the protagonist's narration as a confidence between women convey an explicitly feminine sensibility. By contrast, "The Cigarette Stub," published seventeen years later, presents a male protagonist who consciously experiments with the same notion of the "significant insignificant."

I was invited to the wedding of Micaelita Aránguiz and Bernardo de Meneses, and, being unable to attend, was greatly surprised to learn the following morning—the ceremony had been scheduled for ten o'clock in the evening at the bride's house—that when the bishop of San Juan de Acre asked the bride if she took Bernardo for her husband, she let loose—at the very foot of the altar—

with a resounding and energetic "No!" When the question was repeated with astonishment and elicited yet another negative, the groom, after facing for a quarter of an hour the most ridiculous situation in the world, had no choice but to depart, dissolving the gathering and the engagement at the same time.

Such incidents are not unheard-of; we read of them frequently in the newspapers, but they involve people of humble means, in circles where social conventions don't hamper the frank and spontaneous manifestation of sentiment and the will.

What was peculiar about the scene created by Micaelita was the setting in which it occurred. I could picture it in my mind and was very disappointed not to have witnessed it with my own eyes. I imagined the crowded salon; the carefully chosen guests: the ladies dressed in velvet and silk, with necklaces of precious stones, and with white mantillas on their arms, ready to be put over their heads at the proper moment during the ceremony; men resplendent with medals or sporting military insignias on the front of their frock coats; the bride's mother, richly ornamented, solicitous, busily circulating from group to group and accepting congratulations; the bride's sisters filled with emotion and looking very pretty, the eldest in pink and the youngest in blue, displaying the turquoise bracelets that were gifts from their future brother-in-law; the bishop who was to conduct the ceremony, alternately grave and affable, smiling, deigning to recite polite jokes or discreet praise. In the background one would discern the chapel bedecked with flowers, a flood of white roses from the floor to the little cupola, where spokes of snowlike lilacs and roses converged over artistically arranged green boughs; while on the altar stood the statue of the Virgin, protectoress of the aristocratic mansion, partly veiled by a curtain of orange blossoms, a carload of which were sent from Valencia by the very wealthy businessman Aránguiz, uncle and godfather of the bride, who couldn't come in person because of age and infirmity. These details would be circulated by word of mouth, fueling estimates of the magnificent inheritance that would belong to Micaelita—one more source of happiness for the couple, who were to spend their honeymoon in Valencia. In a group of gentlemen, I pictured the groom, somewhat nervous, slightly pale, biting his mustache distractedly, nodding in acknowledgment of the restrained jokes and the words of flattery addressed to him . . .

And, finally, in the doorway leading to the inner rooms of the house, I see a kind of apparition: the bride, whose features are barely distinguishable through a cloud of tulle, her silk gown rustling as she passes, the antique stones of her nuptial jewelry glistening like dewdrops on her hair . . . The ceremony gets under way now: the couple goes forward, led by the best man and the matron of honor, the pure white figure kneels next to the trim and dapper groom . . . the family crowds up front to get the best view of friends and onlookers, and, amidst the silence and the respectful attention of those present, the bishop poses a question, to which a "No" is fired back, sharp as a shot, solid as a bullet. In my imagination, I note the groom's movements as he squirms, wounded; the mother's rush forward as if to defend and protect her daughter; the insistent repetition of the bishop, expressing his astonishment; the shudder of the congregation; the anxious question that spreads in an instant: "What's going on? What is it? Has the bride taken ill? She says no? Impossible! But can it be? What a story!"

All this, in the context of our social life, constitutes a terrible drama. In the case of Micaelita, it was not only drama but also a puzzle. The reason for her refusal never became known.

Micaelita would say only that she had changed her mind and that she was free to turn back, even at the foot of the altar, as long as "I do" hadn't left her lips. Those well acquainted with her family wracked their brains, inventing unlikely explanations. What was certain was that until the fatal moment, the bride and groom had seemed to be happy and very much in love; and the girlfriends who went in to admire the beautifully dressed bride, moments before the scandal, recounted that she was mad with joy and so thrilled and satisfied that she wouldn't have changed places with anybody. These facts served to obscure further the strange enigma that for a long time was a source of gossip for a vexed society ready to offer the most unfavorable explanations for it.

Three years later—when almost no one remembered what happened at Micaelita's wedding—I ran into her in the spa that was currently in fashion, where her mother was taking the mineral baths. Nothing facilitates friendship like resort life, and Miss Aránguiz became such a close friend of mine that one afternoon, on the way to church, she revealed her secret to me, saying that she allowed me to disclose it because she was certain that no one would believe such a simple explanation.

"It was the silliest thing . . . so silly that I refused to speak about it; people always attribute profound and transcendental causes to events, not noticing that our fate is sometimes determined by trifles, the most unimportant little things . . . But they're little things that mean something, and for some people they mean too much. I'll tell you what happened; and I can't imagine why no one realized, because it happened right there, in front of everybody; only they didn't notice because it was really just in the twinkling of an eye.

"You know that my marriage to Bernardo de Meneses seemed to bring every guarantee for happiness. Besides, I confess that I very much liked my fiancé, more than any man I knew or know; I think I was in love with him. The only thing I regretted was not being able to study his character—some people thought him violent, but around me he always was courteous, deferential, soft as a glove. I feared that he was putting up a front to dupe me and conceal a fierce and sour disposition. A thousand times I cursed the helplessness of a single woman, for whom it is impossible to trail her fiancé's every move, thoroughly investigate the truth, and obtain reliable information, frank to the point of harshness—the only kind of information that would put me at ease. I tried to test Bernardo in many ways, and he did well; his behavior was so correct that I came to believe that I could unreservedly entrust my future and my happiness to him.

"The day of the wedding arrived. When I was putting on the white gown, despite my natural excitement, I noticed once again the superb lace that adorned it and that was a gift from my fiancé. That old genuine Alençon was a family heirloom. It was exquisitely designed, a third of a meter wide—a marvel—beautifully preserved and worthy of a museum. Bernardo had given it to me, extolling its worth, which began to exasperate me, for no matter how much the lace was worth, my intended should believe that I deserved more.

"In that solemn moment, when I saw it set off against the dense satin of my gown, it seemed to me that the delicate design of the lace signified a promise of happiness and that its weave, so fragile and yet so strong, captured two hearts in its tenuous mesh. I was immersed in these musings as I began to walk toward the parlor, where my fiancé waited at the door. As I was rushing to greet him for the last time before belonging to him body and soul, full of joy, the lace got caught on the wrought iron of the door, so unluckily that when I tried to free myself, I heard the distinctive sound of a rip, and I could see that a length of the magnificent trim lay dangling over my skirt. But I saw something else—Bernardo's face, contorted and disfigured by the most vivid rage; his eyes blazing like coals, his mouth already half open to issue a rebuke and an insult . . . He didn't get that far, because he was surrounded by people; but in that brief moment a curtain was parted, exposing a naked soul behind it.

"I must have turned pale; fortunately, the tulle of my veil covered my face. Something cracked and shattered into pieces inside me, and the joy with which I had crossed the threshold of the salon turned into a profound horror. I still saw Bernardo before me with that expression of rage, cruelty, and contempt that I had just glimpsed in his face; this idea took hold of me, and with it came another one: that I couldn't, that I wouldn't give myself to such a man, not then, not ever . . . Nonetheless I kept walking toward the altar, knelt, listened to the bishop's exhortations . . . But when I was asked, the truth sprang to my lips, impetuous and terrible . . .

"That *no* sprang forth without my meaning it to; I was saying it to myself . . . so that all could hear!"

"And why didn't you reveal the reason when it was talked about so much?"

"I repeat: because of the very simplicity of it . . . They would never have believed me. The natural and common-place is never accepted. I preferred to let it be thought there were reasons of the sort they call *serious* . . ."

CHAMPAGNE

Pardo Bazán is more daring in "Champagne" than in many other stories, in both style and theme, because this tale is told by a prostitute to her client, with little narratorial intervention. This was not the first time prostitutes were represented in Spanish fiction; they appear in classic medieval texts, and certainly Pardo Bazán's male contemporaries had represented the figure of the prostitute in their fiction. Nevertheless, a female author's use of a prostitute as framed narrator, without commentary, was probably scandalous. This may explain why "Champagne" was never published in any of the popular journals, unlike the vast majority of Pardo Bazán's stories.

The reproduction of the protagonist's colloquial speech is also unusual. Although Pardo Bazán did indeed record the speech of rural people and of the working classes with a fair degree of verisimilitude elsewhere, rarely did she do so to this extent.

Particularly intriguing is the protagonist's suggestion that if more women told the truth about their feelings, they would be in the same situation that she is in or worse. This striking assertion might recall to the contemporary reader's memory the lines from "Käthe Kollwitz," by the American poet Muriel Rukeyser: "What would happen if one woman told the truth about her life? The world would split open" (The Speed of Darkness *[New York: Random, 1968] 99–105).*

Raimundo Valdés's curiosity was piqued when he saw his evening companion's eyes darken as the cork was popped off the gold-sealed bottle. That shadow of pain or of memories led him to inquire why a woman whose profession it was to be jovial would allow herself to show sadness. That was a luxury reserved for decent women, women who were the owners and mistresses of their hearts and souls.

He begged her to share her secret, and apparently the prostitute happened to be in one of those states of mind when we need to unburden ourselves and so reveal our most intimate story to the first soul we encounter; she drew her hand across her eyes and answered without hesitation or pretension:

"It always makes me sad when a bottle of champagne is opened, because that beverage cost me a lot . . . on my wedding day."

"So you were married before in the Church?" asked Raimundo, with an easy presumptuousness.

"I wish I hadn't been," she answered with obvious unrehearsed candor. "It's because I got married that you see me now the way I am."

"Then your husband is some sort of swindler, a thief?"

"Not in the least. He knows how to manage what he has, and he has thousands. Yes, thousands, or hundreds of thousands."

"By God, woman, that's a lot of money! In that case, didn't he take good care of you? Did he have affairs? Did he beat you?"

"He didn't treat me badly. He didn't beat me and, as far as I know, he didn't get involved with other women. But, my God, have I ever been beaten since then! Truth is, he didn't have time to give me a bad life, or, for that matter, a good one, because we only spent a few hours together as a married couple."

"Hm-m!" Valdés murmured, beginning to sense an interesting tale.

"I'll tell you what happened, sugar. My parents were decent people, but they didn't have a penny. Dad held a low-paying job, and we barely scraped by on his miserable wages. Then my mother died and my father lost his job. And, since he couldn't put food in my mouth or in my brother's and was pretty handsome, he allowed himself to be sweet-talked by a fat-thighed rich woman and took her as his second wife. At first my stepmother acted—well—decently. She didn't treat us stepkids too badly. But as I grew and became a woman and as men began to say things to me on the street, I realized she had it in for me at home. Everything I did was wrong, and she was always spying on me and criticizing. My father turned quiet, and I understood that it hurt him inside to see me mistreated that way.

"The result of all these run-ins was that they decided to find me a husband and get rid of me. By chance they found someone right away. A well-situated specimen, fortyish, proper, respectable, very serious. Anyway, he satisfied even my father, who agreed this was an excellent chance for me. So, they arranged the marriage in secret, and all the details of the wedding, and one day, when I least expected it, it was off to the altar—never mind what I thought about it!"

"And how did the news hit you? Hard, eh?"

"Horrible . . . because I was foolish enough at the time to be head over heels in love—as only girls fall in love, girls though they may look like women on the outside—with a guy in the infantry, a lieutenant, poor as a rat. And I had it in my head that he would be my husband as soon as he became captain. But my father's pleas, advice from my friends, scoldings and even blows from my stepmother—who hardly even let me breathe—had put me into such a state that I didn't dare resist. And so the gifts began to pile in, and the boxes from Madrid full of dresses, and it was off with the lids and on with white ruffles and fastening the crown of orange blossoms[1]— what a sham! Then to the church for the sacrament, and after that the big feast, with friends of the family and the

---

[1] The crown of orange blossoms traditionally symbolizes virginity.

groom's relatives offering toasts, making my head feel like a brass drum, and all the while I felt more like crying than eating anything."

"My dear, so far I find nothing unusual in your story. It's so common to be railroaded into marriage."

"Wait a minute!" she exclaimed, gesturing with her hand. "Now comes the ridiculous part—the real turn of fate. You see, I had never in my life tried champagne . . . They served me my first glass so I could drink to the toast, and after I emptied it, it seemed to me that my spirits had lifted; I wasn't in such despair, and my feeling of dark sorrow was disappearing. I drank the second glass, and the good feeling got even better. Joy spread throughout my body. So I went ahead and drank three, four, five, half a dozen glasses . . .

"The guests made a big joke about this, cheering me on for drinking that way. I drank, hoping to forget—with the champagne—what was to happen to me and what was already happening. All the same, I stopped before getting completely drunk, and all that anyone at the table could tell was that I laughed too loud, that my eyes flashed, and that I was extremely flushed.

"A coach was waiting for us—for my husband and me— to take us to a country house he owned to spend the first week after the wedding. Honey, I don't know if it was the movement of the coach or the fresh air or that I was three sheets to the wind, plain and simple. The fact is that as soon as I found myself alone with the gentleman and he began whispering sweet nothings into my ear, my blood heated, my tongue loosened, and I started to tell him about the lieutenant, that the lieutenant was the only one I loved, and I went on and on, the lieutenant this and the lieutenant that: I had married against my will and would take revenge and beat my husband to death. Just rubbish, mind you, just the things wine makes people say when they're not used to drinking. And my husband, paler than a dead man, ordered the coach to turn around, and he took me back to my house then and there. Or that is what they told me later, because I was so tipsy, you know, I had no idea what was going on."

"And your husband never let you come back?"

"Never. It seems I said some really dreadful things. You see, it was the damned champagne talking."

"And your family? Were they willing to take you back?"

"Ha! My stepmother insulted me horribly, and my father went around crying everywhere. I realized it was better for me to take to the streets, and to hell with it!"

"And what of the lieutenant?"

"The lieutenant! As soon as he found out about my wedding, he got another girlfriend and married her in a wink and a whistle."

"You know, you really had some bad luck there."

"Bad luck for sure. But I think that if all women spoke their minds—as I did because of the champagne—a lot of them would be worse off than me."

"And does your husband support you? It's the law."

"Bah! I've already been told that by a lawyer 'I had' and may the devil take him to court! How can I ask my husband to support me after the way I let him down? Come on, give me more champagne. Now I can drink whatever I want. My lips have no more secrets to let out."

THE LOOK

Like "First Love," "Memento," and "My Suicide," "The Look" is told by a male narrator. But the narrator's stance is not to be identified with that of the author. Notice how this nameless, successful businessman is characterized negatively by his own actions, thoughts, and the language he uses.

In many ways, this story serves as an excellent representation of women's constantly being placed "on the market," as Luce Irigaray puts it ("Women on the Market," This Sex Which Is Not One, trans. Catherine Porter [Ithaca: Cornell UP, 1985] 170-92). The inextricable linking here of the look to issues of sexual domination also anticipates contemporary ideas.

While attending to business for a large industrial concern in which I had an interest, occasionally I had to travel to M***, where no one knew me and where I knew no one. During my brief stays there, at the best inn in town, I was able to admire from my window the beauty of a lady who lived in the house across the street. From my observation point it was possible to examine her boudoir in a most indiscreet way, and I would look on her beauty as she sat at her dressing table laden with jars and perfume atomizers, studying herself in the mirror, combing her regal auburn tresses, taking pleasure in flattering them with her brush, teasing and forming them around her pale, perfect face. She smiled with satisfaction when she had finished subduing the waves of her hair with the last rhinestone comb, repeatedly smoothing the templelike edifice with a long and delicate hand. After this she lightly touched the powder puff to her face; put the final touches on her eyebrows; polished her nails interminably with coral paste; tried on hats, bows, belts, flower hairpins, and lace, which she gathered around her neck. In sum, she consecrated long hours to the worship of her own beauty. As I was glued to the window by the provocative spectacle, my blood boiling from so profaning the privacy of a seductive woman, a different curiosity was born in me: the urge to know her story, in which, no doubt, there would be passionate episodes, joys, sorrows, memories.

And so I trembled one evening when I heard her name spoken at our business roundtable discussion—*she* was being talked about . . . I became aroused, like the hunter when he senses his prey stir in the bushes. The conversation was led by the traveling jewelry salesman, a Frenchman, Monsieur Lamouche, who said that he planned to stop by the house of the "belle Madame—" (he uttered the last name, but I will not yield it up to public knowledge) to offer his "wares," hoping for a big sale.

"Don't even think about it!" a fellow diner objected, a young man from a neighboring town who had come to pass the day merrily in M***. "I know Tilde's husband all too well—she's my distant cousin, I don't quite know how we're related. No sooner had he given his wife her wedding jewels[1] than all extravagance ended. Yes, in truth he is stingier than an ant."

"Can it be," the traveler observed in his rudimentary Spanish, "that the husband not gets along with his lady, who is *très* pretty and will surely *tromper* him, *allons tout naturally?*"

"If only that were so!" the young man sighed jokingly. "Were Tilde so inclined, I'd be number one on the list, even if her legal owner broke my crown for it. On the contrary! Tilde has never given the slightest cause for gossip. I don't deny that she is fully absorbed in her own beauty. Her only passion is putting on makeup, dressing up. It gives her such pleasure to see other women fume over her elegance—more that even than to make a conquest. Bah! If she had transgressed at all, even in a single look, we would all know. In small towns these things can't be hidden. And a woman who will give a man a look will give him everything. I tell you again, and anyone

---

[1] Traditionally, the set of wedding jewels consisted of a necklace, earrings, brooches, and a bracelet.

would tell you the same, that Tilde is not only irreproach-able but as cold and unassailable as ice."

The other diners confirmed the young man's asser-tions.

"Well then," insisted the Frenchman, who never lost sight of his business, "if she so loves her *toilette*, I do have some delightful things."

"A waste of time! Her husband will never soften. He's a swine! To have a woman like that and subject her to such a meager monthly allowance for clothing! He de-serves . . ."

At the close of the conversation, which went on end-lessly, my heart began to beat faster and my veins to buzz: a strange idea had just occurred to me. The young man and the other guests went to the theater, and now that I was alone with Monsieur Lamouche, who enjoyed my conversation because I spoke French easily, I offered him my proposition. Instead of refusing—as I had feared—he accepted and even applauded it, overjoyed, making a gesture in the air as if to clap me on the belly.

"Oh! *Ma foi!* Very nice, very Spanish . . . Like in the romances, *sapristi!* I only ask that you . . . be prudent . . . do not compromise me."

I should mention that the traveler was an old acquaintance of mine and that he respected me as a serious businessman. He was quite capable of distinguishing the honest person from the swindler in that dangerous profession of his, being a trader in unnecessary articles that everyone wants to own and no one wants to pay for. Refusing the deposit I tried to give him, he placed in my hands two black sharkskin cases filled with his best jewels. With the cases under my arm and my heart in my mouth, I climbed the staircase in the house that belonged to Tilde, the woman I was finally going to see up close, perhaps alone, in that very room, the temple of her beauty. This was my sole intention: to gaze upon her, to breathe in her amber-scented breath . . . and, perhaps, our hands would touch lightly for a moment as we handled the jewels. I was announced, and indeed I did enter her boudoir, by now dizzy and weak, feverish.

Tilde was wrapped in a robe I was already familiar with—a robe of soft gray silk, pleated and covered by such a quantity of golden lace that the cloth itself was barely visible. In close proximity the deity was even more divine! In that lottery even those who came near the winning number won! I don't know what luminous and intoxicating atmosphere enveloped her; I don't know what subtle, delicate exhalations came from her young body, perfumed, free and loose like the bodies of Hellenic statues in their many-pleated garments. Disconcerted, but maintaining self-control, I opened the cases and presented the selections. Out came bracelets and trims, chains and pendants, double-arced rings, strings of pearls, and diamond pins, all of which she picked up, held in her hands, tried on, pinned on herself, fastened around her neck with squeals and exclamations of delight. Everything pleased her; she looked at herself in the mirror; she let her bejeweled hands play in the light coming through the window—the revealing, indiscreet window. She didn't see me; for her I was the display case, less than secondary—quite incidental.

At last, from among these diverse temptations, one stronger than the others took hold of her feminine soul: her gaze was captured by a necklace of diamonds and pearls, long a yearning of hers, no doubt, and whose absence from her jewelry case had distressed her a thousand times; her eyes were now suddenly sad, and her voice turned opaque and timid as she asked:

"How much?"

I shot out the price—I had taken care to inform myself—and I saw her dark pupils, aglow with desire and greed, fade. She didn't have the money for the coveted jewel! Just then a spark of will flared up inside me. I didn't reason; I murmured, with the hiss of the serpent beneath the tree of evil:

"If Madame would like the necklace . . . there are a thousand ways. We offer easy terms. Immediate payment isn't necessary—a certain amount per month, for example . . ."

She raised her head slowly and looked at me for the first time. Her fine-tuned ear, her sagacity of an Eve accustomed to adoration, detected in my stammered reply something beyond the phrases I uttered. The tremblings of a soul filtered their way through my vulgar commercial offers just as water seeps through the unglazed clay of a water jug. With my eyes I responded to hers, which questioned without meaning to. The daggers of our souls, honed and cruel, crossed in the form of a long and meaningful look. "She hasn't strayed, not even with a look . . ." "A woman who will give a man a look will give him everything." I recalled the young man's phrase, and as I did so, I was bedazzled even more by the diabolical light that blazed up inside me, from the depths of my being, for I was a passionate, self-indulgent man in the prime of life. And certain that the words of an entire dictionary could not add meaning to Tilde's look, I leaned over and simultaneously stretched out my arms and the necklace to her, imperiously fastening it about her throat, trembling as my fingers tangled in the regal head of auburn hair, alive and electric . . .

Tilde cost me rather dearly. A jewel per visit. Nonetheless, I will never regret those thousands of francs because, when I returned years later to M***, I found out that the beautiful woman—ever beautiful, because she seemed to possess a secret that preserved her beauty in ice—still passed as unassailable, a woman who not even with a look . . .

THE KEY

Pardo Bazán's female characters are not exempt from her acerbic criticism, as "The Key" demonstrates. The narrative perspective is manipulated in an ironic way; while the protagonist is bewildered by the behavior of his uncle's new wife, to most readers her motives will seem clear from the start. But by the end of the story, it becomes much more difficult to identify Tolina's reasons for marrying don Juan. Thus even those readers who feel they have immediately grasped "the key" to the enigma are tricked just as poor Calixto is.

The author has imbued this short story with a curious intertextuality. First, the protagonist's odd name, Calixto, echoes that of the central male character of Fernando de Rojas's 1499 work Comedia de Calisto y Melibea, *or* La Celestina, *which relates the tragedy of a pair of star-crossed lovers in the style of Shakespeare's later* Romeo and Juliet. *Melibea repulses Calisto just as Pardo Bazán's Calixto rejects Antolina's advances. Furthermore, the name of Calixto's uncle, Nepomuceno, is the same as that of a character in Clarín's 1891 novel* Su único hijo *(His Only Son). Clarín's character, also an uncle and mentor, is an amoral schemer who spends a large part of his niece's fortune under the guise of protecting her investments. Both he and Pardo Bazán's Nepomuceno share the Spanish name for Saint John of Nepomuk, bishop of Prague and patron saint of confessors, who in 1393 supposedly was thrown off*

a bridge to his death when he refused to reveal the details
of Queen Sophia's confession to King Wenceslaus IV. (More
modern scholarship suggests that the saint died a victim of
political intrigue.) In both cases, Pardo Bazán has taken
well-known literary characters and transferred their out-
standing features to her own characters but of the opposite
sex. We might wonder whether she is offering her readers
a teasing challenge: to consider the implications of her idi-
osyncratic gender-bending textual allusions.

Calixto Silva discovered—on returning from a trip that
had lasted four months—that his uncle and mentor, that
excellent don Juan Nepomuceno, to whom he owed his
education, his career, the conservation and growth of his
estate, and the most solicitous concern for his health,
was getting married. And to whom? To none other than
Tolina Cortés, that harebrained woman who had so per-
sistently tried to trap him, Calixto, through flirtation,
schemes, and other deviltry that actually served only to
drive him away. Now, as he remembered them in the
light of the news of his uncle's wedding, they filled him
with disgust and fear.

His uncle had neither consulted him nor seemed disposed to listen to his opinions regarding the marriage. So
Calixto had to resign himself to it. His only protest was
to express his wish to leave the house and live alone; but
don Juan said no.

"Don't give me a headache! More than my nephew,
you're my son; and if I ever have children, I won't love

them more than I love you. The girl"—that is what don Juan called his wife-to-be—"will treat me as a widower who has a child. That's it. Until the day you marry, all will continue as before."

Calixto went to the wedding ceremony, trembling inside with rage as he looked at the soft garland of orange blossoms that crowned the bold forehead of the diabolical creature beneath the veiling cloud of tulle. How had the little serpent managed to wrap her coils around the honest old man's heart? What art, what tricks, what black magic had she used? No doubt, the very same that Calixto remembered as the organ poured out its vibrant torrent of deep and sonorous notes and as a graceful figure at the altar, enveloped in silks that mysteriously increased her height, articulated a muted "I do," an "I do" as white as the silk itself.

The galling enigma preoccupied Calixto, and he thought about his uncle's wife incessantly; she was in the house all day and all night. He resolved to keep an eye on her, to guard don Juan's honor, allowing no one to make a mockery of don Juan with impunity. This noble and firm determination was his justification for remaining in the house. He would keep his eyes and ears open: Tolina had better watch her step or else . . .

Tolina employed the most Machiavellian hypocrisy: her conduct was irreproachable. She attended a few social events, showing only limited enthusiasm for them. She dressed and adorned her person modestly. With the even and cheerful temperament the girl displayed around her husband, she was really more a daughter than a wife to him. She cared for him, amused and flattered him, showed him respect in public, spoiled him at home, and—Calixto had to admit this to himself—don Juan enjoyed true happiness. Doting on the kind, sweet little woman, he incessantly repeated sugary phrases:

"Isn't she adorable, Calixto? Find one like this for yourself. No one should die before discovering such joy."

Calixto, frowning, held back his reservations and dark suspicions.

Really, it could not go on this way! Sooner or later, Tolina would show her true colors. If she was behaving herself for now, there must be a reason . . . Bah! He continued to watch her with malicious vigilance. Tolina, affectionate, somewhat hurt though not uttering a word, tried not to irritate or intrude on the nephew whom don Juan called son, and the nephew, indifferent to Tolina as a woman, could not stop worrying about her motives as a wife. Why did she maintain her husband's decorum so consistently and in so dignified a manner? Why did she give no cause for suspicion, none at all? Instead of making Calixto happy—we are not very logical creatures!—this was eating at him inside. It is only human: he who predicts the worst is always mortified when he is not proved right.

The cause for Tolina's good behavior . . . a sudden radiance illuminated Calixto as he guessed it. It was so clear! How could he not have understood before! What the young woman wanted and had assured herself possession of with such art was the old man's fortune, his considerable inheritance. It was calculation that protected her virtue and the happiness of her trusting spouse. Sweet little Tolina Cortés belonged to the phalanx of calculating women, the knowing phalanx that waits and prepares the lamp for the following evening.

When he hit on this key to the problem, Calixto felt doubly satisfied. Recognizing mean and greedy instincts in Tolina Cortés, his pessimism was satisfied. His generosity moved him to rejoice in renouncing the inheritance he had never coveted. And, to face sooner what might come, one day during a lull in the conversation he said to don Juan:

"Uncle, no one is assured of being alive tomorrow. I've had an inheritance since I came of age. Why don't you make arrangements and leave your money to Aunt Antolina? She deserves it, and it's fair."

"She deserves it, and it's fair," the old man repeated, mimicking his nephew. "I would leave her the kingdoms of Spain . . . but let me tell you, she isn't interested, she won't hear of money. When I spoke to her about it, she was so vexed and pained that she became ill. It's the only disagreement we've had. She demands that you be my heir. Why such astonishment? Had you thought she married me for money? She? Tolinita?"

And the old man's kind face, ruddy through the halo of gray beard and hair, beamed with pleasure.

"So be it; but I won't allow such foolishness and injustice," Calixto declared. "What you leave to me will be for her."

"You won't be able to persuade her. She doesn't want it. She's better than an angel!"

After this conversation, Calixto's behavior changed. Instead of spying on Tolina, he avoided her. The suspicion he now had was deeper, more piercing, more disturbing than before. His spirit was invaded by a sadness, a disquiet that knew no limits. He lost his appetite and could not sleep. Late one evening, noticing that he was missing his wallet, in which he had left several bills, he went down to the villa's garden at an odd hour to see whether he might find it there; on his hands and knees he searched the plants until he reached some bushes that hid a stone bench from view. He stopped. A woman, seated on the bench, was kissing a red object.

Taken aback, without realizing what he was saying, he stammered, "What are you doing here?"

"And you?" she replied, serene.

"I . . . I . . . I was looking for my wallet."

"Here it is. I found it a few moments ago."

Smiling, Tolina held out the wallet of red Russian leather. Calixto didn't take it. He felt himself turning pale, and his voice stuck in his throat.

"What is it?" Coming closer, the lady placed the wallet near the immobile hands that would not take it. "Come," she added with a mixture of melancholy and malice. "Take your money . . . You know that I'm not going to keep it."

Calixto responded—without rising from the ground—by throwing his arms around a body that trembled with passion and triumph . . . Tolina, bending over, said:

"At last! It took long enough . . . Blind, you're blind!"

A heavy step was heard in the sand . . . Calixto stood up . . . don Juan was approaching.

"We were looking for this wallet," a radiant Tolina explained, holding it high in the air. "Would you believe Calixto was almost touching it, and he couldn't see it? And it was right before his eyes! That's the way it always is: we insist on not seeing the things that are most evident. Here, nephew," she continued, slipping the wallet into his pocket with charming familiarity, "don't lose it again, for it's worth quite a bit . . ."

Calixto departed the next morning, leaving behind a

brief but affectionate farewell letter. He said he needed to travel for an extended period of time, to complete his education, to see the world. When she learned of the letter—it had made don Juan furious when he read it ("Devil take the boy! What kind of nonsense is that!")— Tolina said nothing.

Lately her health declined, and though don Juan takes her to spas and the examination rooms of celebrated doctors, it is still not known what exactly it is she suffers from. Nerves, most likely. Nerves, another mystery with no key.

THE WEDDING

Published twelve years after "Torn Lace," "The Wedding" returns to the earlier story's conceit of the bride whose orientation toward her marriage and husband changes completely on the very day of her wedding, and within the span of a moment. The sympathetic treatment of female sexuality echoes that found in several other stories of Pardo Bazán's, such as "Memento" and "Champagne." The protagonist's point of view is presented almost exclusively here; the reader is privileged with not only the knowledge of Regina's secret erotic desire but also the experience of it, when Regina gazes at the light playing across the eyes and mustache of the man she wants. But how are we to interpret the "happy ending" that distinguishes this story from "Torn Lace," "Memento," or "Champagne"? The "open" ending invites us to speculate about the chances that bride and groom will find satisfaction in this marriage.

It was a splendid, springlike day. The people who were crammed into the omnibus headed for Viveros were in the best of moods and ravenously hungry after a morning of hustle-bustle, excitement, and fresh air. They had high expectations for the banquet: the groom was quite rich and generous, and he was mad about his bride. Nicasio the silversmith knew for a fact and had confided

91

in doña Fausta the dyer and her daughters: there would be champagne and lobster and even a surprise, a dish worthy of a marquis and called *faw graw*.

And Nicasio wasn't mistaken. The owner of several small hardware factories and of the best store on Atocha Street, don Elías had lost count of the years he had wooed the disdainful Regina, daughter of doña Andrea, the headmistress of the children's school in the Santa Cruz plaza. Regina was a fashionable blonde, with more of the ways of a proper young lady than most, so very nicely educated, and a dreamer by nature. Because she had read quite a bit—history, novels, verse, and ditties about love—she had an unquenchable enthusiasm for the theater—not for light comedy or licentious plays but for tragedy and serious and sentimental drama. It would have been an exaggeration to call her beautiful, but there was a certain attractiveness about her—an elegance, a way of behaving above her social sphere—and the lines of her body were admirably trim, enhanced by delicate and simple attire in the French style. She did not pass unnoticed anywhere, and she was envied by some and imitated by others.

Despite the campaign by her mother, who was beside herself with joy at the prospect of a suitor such as don Elías, Regina had resisted for years before accepting him. She gave no explanation. She did not want to . . . don't anyone speak to her of such a thing . . . she was mistress of her own mind . . . she had no ambition . . . she was not for sale . . . and other such arguments. She was not known to have any other suitor, and this is what drove her mother to distraction. "But after all, she loves no one! For all my watching, I have seen no ships on the horizon!"

But we can observe only material facts . . . Hearts do not have windows in them. Regina had been resolute in her nay-saying because she remained unconvinced that her French teacher, a poor young gentleman who was as handsome as Apollo, had not noticed her beyond greeting her respectfully when she entered and departed from the classroom. He was the man, to be sure! Just one word from *him!* Secretly and without any conspicuous display, Regina suffered the long and cruel torments of love's fever. One day, when she was cursing more than ever the lot of women that does not permit them to reveal their longings, regardless of how deeply felt, she observed the dashing teacher discreetly pass a note to a hunchbacked student, the only daughter of a millionaire moneylender. Sleepless nights and days without appetite ensued; there were involuntary tears and even fits of pique: the defense of an ideal that refuses to die . . . A month later, suddenly and without warning, Regina announced to her mother that she was willing to marry don Elías. She took solace in the fact that no one knew of her ill-fated, thwarted dreams . . . She had been able to conceal them; it was as though her humiliation never existed, since not even doña Andrea, who had spied on her daughter continually, had suspected her. They were a treasure she would keep for herself: her extinguished love, her disillusionment, a dove whose white wings were broken and bloodied . . .

The omnibus was already drawing to a halt at Viveros Plaza. Luxuriously attired in black satin,[1] the bride started to step down, but before the groom could offer her his hand, a handsome man offered his. It was Damián Antiste, the schoolteacher himself, her dream in the flesh, the true author of the union between the starry-eyed young lady and the classic, exemplary Madrid industrialist . . . How was it that Damián was there? Regina was quite certain that he had not been at the church for the wedding. No doubt he feigned a chance meeting with doña Andrea or don Elías and they had invited him. What was undeniable was that he was there and that he might dine at her side . . . or across from her. Regina remembered that the moneylender had withdrawn his hunchbacked daughter from the school and placed her under lock and key, and she thought Damián might have abandoned his ambitious

---

[1] Until about the middle of the twentieth century, it was not unusual for Spanish brides to wear black.

plans. All this came to her in a flash. The terribly gentle touch of the teacher's hand pressing hers as he held it and the sensation of his devouring eyes abolished all feelings but the bitter pleasure of her triumph. Damián's gaze was bold, undisguised, protracted. He scrutinized Regina, truly beautiful at that moment behind the white veil gathered into clouds over her glowing hair with its coquettish waves. She was bedecked with orange blossoms in their waxen green foliage; resplendent on her ears were two droplets of water—a jewel worth a thousand duros in each lobe, an extravagance of her splendid and enthusiastic consort. "Today he finds me attractive," thought Regina, trembling with pleasure. She averted her eyes; but the magnet of her soul pulled them again toward the teacher, who continued to devour her with his own. Oh, that look, two months ago! But why *now?* No doubt it was the effect of her gown, the tulle, the jewels . . . Damián *hadn't really seen her* until that moment. Women have these notions; they believe in the irresistible powers of adornment, of clothes, of finery, and they destroy themselves in the pursuit of them! If Damián had seen her as radiant, as decked out as she was at this moment, he would no doubt have contemplated her then as he did now. But Damián had not known that she was pretty or that she had been pining for him . . . Like dammed water that has suddenly found an outlet, Regina's illusions flowed. It was long-standing passion satisfying itself without restraint, without regard for decency or modesty . . . Fortunately, the groom had hurried off to speak with the innkeeper about his orders and to see whether the splendid lunch would be served soon.

Regina's friends removed her veil and decided that they would play hide-and-seek until it was time to sit at the table. The wedding party scattered along the paths at the water's edge, paths that were perfumed by the last of the lilacs and by early blossoms of the fragrant white syringas. The scent from those Madrid flowers in the warm dry air was unsettling. The delicate, young, and yielding foliage of the shrubs obscured the tall tree trunks and became a kind of moving perfumed screen in front of the stream. This bourgeois oasis was poetry; the distant notes from the street organ playing tunes from popular zarzuelas for a few tips, even they were poetry. Rolling up the train of her magnificent dress as she felt her youth rise boiling inside her, the bride set an example by scampering away. Damián followed her. No one noticed them, or if her girlfriends did, they felt like accomplices in the matter: let the bride laugh, let her have a little diversion. Serious duties would be hers soon enough!

Damián quickly caught up with the bride. Smiling, he cornered her in a thicket of verdant young trees that offered a refuge from the sun. He drew near, and Regina savored the strangely divine pleasure of seeing close, very close, the face she had been dreaming about. Now, so near, so dominating, it appeared different, with the sun sparkling in his eyes and with the color of his mustache changing in the light. The bride swooned, and the young man threw his arms around her waist and began to murmur confused words; the eternal song that takes hold of souls . . . At first Regina listened, drinking in his speech, which made her dizzy and intoxicated at the same time. But then . . . What was this man saying? Regina pulled back, shocked by what she heard. Inept, clumsy, he continued:

"Don't deny that you wanted me, that you yearned for me back in school. Don't deny it. For I knew it. Why, I noticed from the very moment it started."

The bride's countenance at first showed amazement, then embarrassment, then infinite contempt, then profound anger. The swine! So he knew! And all the while he was writing notes to the millionairess! Not a single sign of gratitude, not a single consoling or sympathetic word to her! He let her perish! He let her marry another! And now . . . the swine.

The word rose to her lips, which were white with fury. "Swine!" she shouted.

Slowly, without turning back, she left the thicket and

walked toward the dining room. There she would find her fiancé, her husband. And he was there indeed, giving orders, indicating seats at the table.

"Elías!" she said affectionately. "You'll make sure I get to sit next to you, won't you?"

It was the first time she had spoken to him like this . . . Everybody remarked that during the luncheon—a luncheon that made for memories—she was tender and ingratiating, and the groom was out of his mind with joy.

THE FOREWARNED

"The Forewarned" is thematically and stylistically typical of Pardo Bazán's later work. We see the figure of the woman who has been seduced and abandoned, a commonplace in nineteenth-century literature, especially Victorian fiction, and one that Pardo Bazán herself used in many of her works. But rather than focus on the high drama of the situation, as authors like Hardy and Dickens do, she presents the "wronged woman" in a way that implicitly denounces hypocritical cultural attitudes toward sexuality. She melds this social criticism with a concern for "the psychology of the moment," which in many ways presages the modernist experiments of such writers as Katherine Mansfield and Virginia Woolf. This direct representation of thought is particularly intriguing in its focus on the resentment that a member of one sex has developed, with justification or not, toward the entire opposite sex and the curious ways in which that resentment can be unexpectedly softened.

The road was hard with frost. Puddles left over from the last rain were covered with layers of ice that, had it been day, would have glistened like mirrors. But it was the deep of night, limpid and glacial. The indigo heavens, the jewel box of the Northern Hemisphere, sparkled: the five gems of Cassiopeia; Pegasus, the perfect brooch which a luminous chain links to Andromeda and Perseus; the lapidary rain of the Pleiades; the delicate Corona Borealis; the Chariot made of splendid diamonds; dazzling Vega; the dusty light of the Dragon; the Milky Way flowing from the white breast of Juno. A beautiful night for the astronomer who through the lens of his telescope takes in portions of the sidereal universe and, studying them, is overcome by the serene harmony of creation as he ponders distant worlds inhabited by unknown beings, beings whose mysteries are not amenable to the power of reason. Beautiful too for the dreamer who, gazing through a broad window by a fireplace with logs ablaze, lets his fancy wander into space, recalling the alabaster verses of Leopardi and the bitter and divine prose of Nietzsche. Black night! Tragic for that solitary person who, pierced by the cold, carefully proceeds down the ice-encrusted ribbon of road, dodging those dangerous mirrors of frozen puddles.

It is a young woman. The clothes that cover but do not protect her reveal the roundness of her stomach, the nearness of a child's birth . . . For many months Agustina has lived hunched over, wanting to hide her misfortune from prying and malevolent eyes, but now she stands erect, fearless. No one sees her. She has fled from her village, her home, and she feels relieved not to have to cover herself or hide her burden. Surely the stars look upon her with compassion, or, at the very least, with indifference. They are so distant!

What scorn, what mockery, what reproach had fallen on her in her village when her mistake became known! It was the second time a young woman had erred in that honest place. The first one had thrown herself into a well, from which they extracted her body, five months pregnant. Agustina remembered that they had got the woman out with hooks and ropes; she remembered how the woman's temple was broken and how her hair clung to her livid face. Agustina dreamt about the drowned woman for nights on end. When her own misfortune was confirmed and she thought of death as the solution, the image of the woman's broken temple and livid face kept Agustina from putting into action her desperate decision. Some Franciscan missionaries had come to town then and Agustina, bathed in tears, had confessed.

"Your sin is great," the friar had said, "but your thoughts are worse. You must not die, nor should the child die because of your sin. Suffer with patience, wait until your term, then take this letter to Madrid. The gentleman to whom it is addressed will arrange for you to be admitted to the Maternity Home."

The day was close at hand. Saying good-bye to no one—not even to her parents, who cursed her instead of pitying her—Agustina made a bundle with two shirts and a petticoat. She put a few pesetas in a canvas bag. With the letter in her bosom, she left at dusk through the corral door, before the lads who knew of her misfortune—friends of the one who had caused it—were out and about. Instead of standing by her, the coward had vanished from the town. It was Christmas Eve. It would be strange if the men had not gone out to their partying. Agustina hurried. Shame put wings on her feet.

She had been walking for two hours, and she still had five kilometers to go before reaching Madrid. Exhaustion began to overtake her. She was not used to such exercise, and the cold chilled her to the marrow. Besides, she was afraid. The road was so deserted!

The gray barren plain surrounded her, showing no sign of habitation. Oaks twisted into grotesque figures: deformed dwarfs or dogs hunched over, waiting to pounce and bite. The silence was majestic and terrifying. The fugitive was hungry, with that provident hunger that tells those who will be mothers that they must nourish two beings. In her haste, she had not taken even a crust of bread from her home.

She wanted to weep, and two or three times stopped to cry out loud, as though someone could hear her, "Dear God!" "Mother!" Though her mother, hardened as she was, had treated her worse even than her father . . .

Agustina was overwhelmed by weakness, by the tempta-
tion to throw herself to the ground and sleep. Perhaps
sleep would alleviate all her suffering. She might enter a
state of beatitude: memories of those last months, during which, infallibly, on awakening, she would have the
illusion that her misfortune had been only a nightmare.
She would feel her belly and yet not believe it existed . . .
Oh, if only it were so! No one would take advantage of
her or fool her again! No man would touch her without
getting what he deserved!

Her feet, poorly clad, suddenly slipped on the glassy
surface of a puddle. She swayed and fell backward, face
up, and lay in the road, knocked senseless by the brutal
blow.

Ten minutes later the jingling and rolling of a carriage
was heard. Lanterns approached, and the scrawny horse
that uncertainly pulled the vehicle balked before the
body that blocked its way. Surprised, the driver stopped
the coach and looked down. Well, he would have to get
down, help the drunkard. It was no drunkard, but a
woman. Even worse.

Women! No one hated them as much as the rural
doctor who had been urgently called to Madrid that fear-
ful night. The blow he had suffered from his fiancée's
jilting him, her deciding three days before the wedding

103

not to go through with it, then marrying another man in less than a month—that blow had resulted first in a nervous fever that left its mark on his sallow face and then in a profound misanthropy. Intellectual, sentimental, and highly ambitious when he was in love, the doctor had had his wings clipped by disillusionment. It caused him a humiliation of the kind that makes us doubt ourselves forever. It trapped him in that dull little village where he vegetated like a monk, performing a penance of sadness and solitude for the sin of another—something that happens more commonly than is thought. Only out of strict necessity had he undertaken the trip. And now this nuisance on the road. A female!

He took a lantern from the carriage and held it to the unconscious woman's face. He was surprised. She was young and pretty. Her features seemed made of wax, delicate and gentle. Alone, and lost at this hour! An attack? A crime? He tried to lift her . . . A weak whimper revealed that there was life . . .

"What is wrong with you? Are you ill?" the doctor asked, holding her up.

The response was another whimper. It was one of suffering, unmistakable suffering.

"Are you hurt?"

The young woman sat up with difficulty. She seemed disoriented and could not understand why she was there, why a stranger was interrogating her. But memory soon returned, and with it the awareness of pain. Her right arm refused to move. It hung loosely, and a strange feeling of paralysis crept to her shoulder.

"I think my arm is broken," she said.

The doctor felt, searching. She was right!

"Where were you going? Where are you from?"

Agustina looked at the man who spoke to her and so energetically protected her. She saw a face consumed by melancholy, an unkempt beard, eyes in which compassion battled with apathy. It was not easy for her to explain, unless she did it with the sudden and total frankness of someone who is abandoned, someone who is afraid of nothing because all has been lost, someone like Agustina. The country girl, tired of dissembling and lying to her family and to an entire village, could not keep silent. She could not hide anything from the stranger who had come to her aid. She spoke between sobs, without stopping, even without shame or confusion, like one who tells a soul that has known misfortune of misfortunes greater still. She told him her story in a few heartrending phrases.

"Get in the carriage. Cover yourself with the blanket. I will take you to the hospital," he said.

The carriage had rolled down the road for a quarter of an hour, slowly, because the scrawny horse was also slipping on the ice, when Agustina, feeling infinitely grateful, supported, saved, reached for the doctor's hand with her left arm and kissed it, without knowing what she was doing. He trembled. It had been so long since he had felt the contact of feminine lips, and then only in dreams! The young woman, once the moment of elation had passed, was ashamed, confused. What had she done, dear mother! She had kissed a man, she who had sworn never to touch even a hair of one! She, the woman who had learned from experience, the scalded cat, who had undergone so cruel and final an apprenticeship! But was it really a man who sat thus beside her, displaying so much charity, so much thoughtfulness? No; not a man, a saint. A saint like the ones you see at the altar.

Suddenly the doctor turned the carriage and started to travel in the opposite direction.

"We are closer to my house than to Madrid. It is urgent to take care of that arm for you. If we get to Madrid late, we may waste hours. I must examine the fracture and take care of it. You are coming to my house. You shall have everything you need there."

And even as he was speaking these words to a woman, the disillusioned, disconsolate man, the misogynist, was thinking, "She is not a woman. She is a victim, a martyr . . ."

Under the blanket that half warmed and half covered

them, the urgings of youth and the need to love were beginning to surface, laughing in the face of bitter experience.

The stars, growing brighter as the night progressed, would never know. They are so distant! So far away!

CASTAWAYS

In "Castaways," Pardo Bazán echoes the strong criticism she leveled, in essays like "La educación del hombre y la de la mujer" (Men's and Women's Education) and "La mujer española" (The Women of Spain), at the traditional lack of formal education and job training provided to Spanish women. She dramatizes the consequence of an education that prepares women only for domesticity: the wrenching conflict experienced by many between the need for economic survival and the maintenance of an intransigent standard of feminine virtue. The female protagonists of this story are almost entirely without agency. Their lack of agency is reflected even in the linguistic structure of the story: they are virtually never referred to by their proper names, their discourse is presented only indirectly, and the verbs of which they are subjects are rarely true "action verbs."

It is the hour when great cities acquire a mysterious beauty. The work and activity of the day are done. Pedestrians move slowly through the streets, where the refreshing waters of the afternoon wash-downs have receded. Lights widen their clear eyes, though it is not yet night. The amethyst-tinged strawberry tones of twilight envelop the monumental views in a transparent mist flushed with ardor. Ends of tree-lined boulevards adorned with their garlands of green grow gray in the dusk. Flowering acacias overflow with fragrance, suggesting languid dreams, delicious illusions. The fragrance oppresses the heart somewhat, but also uplifts it. Carriages pass by more briskly because the horses are grateful for the coolness of the sunset. The women who occupy them seem more beautiful, tranquil, and relaxed, their features now blurred in the half-light, now accentuated by the glowing circle of a streetlamp or elegant boutique.

Flower girls pass . . . they offer their merchandise, giving away the best of it for free: the perfume, the color, gifts for the senses.

Tempted by the flowers, women make eloquent movements of greed, and if they are too poor to satisfy their whims, we pity them.

And this happened to some shipwrecked women, adrift in the sea of Madrid, about to drown, their eyes fixed on heaven with the sensation of falling into an abyss. Mother and daughters had been in residence in Madrid for over a month and still wore rigorous mourning for the father, who had not even left them enough to pay for it. Debts, yes, plenty of debts.

How could it be that such a hardworking man, a man of pure habits, a family man, should bequeath ruin to his loved ones? Ah! The intelligent pharmacist, stranded in a

109

small town, had been determined to pay tribute to science. It was not enough to set up a pharmacy with all the latest discoveries; he had to stock it with rare and costly medicines: he wanted nothing modern to be missing; he wanted to be up-to-date. "How embarrassing if don Opropio, the doctor, were to prescribe one of these medicines popular today and I did not have it in my establishment! And I would be responsible if the patient got worse or died because I did not have at hand what he needed!"

So everything came to the small-town pharmacy—collections of French and German formulas—and it was a disaster. Don Opropio did not prescribe such delicacies, nor would the townspeople have bought them if he had. One could say that illnesses work closely with their environment and that in villages people come down only with ailments curable by rubs, mallow flowers, leeches, and poultices. Try telling a country bumpkin that "his blood is low in minerals" or that "his arteries have hardened," and dare suggest a radium treatment more expensive than gold and jewelry. It cannot be. There are first- and third-class illnesses, some for the rich and others for the poverty-stricken. Anyway, the pharmacist died of the most common jaundice, his new remedies powerless to save him; ruined, he died leaving behind a wife and two children in poverty. The pharmacy and the medicines barely paid the outstanding bills, and the three women castaways, both humiliated by the disaster and buoyed by hope, moved to the capital with the proceeds from their humble household effects.

The first days they went about stupefied. This Madrid, what magnificence! What grandeur, dignity! Money must be very easy to earn in Madrid! So many stores! So many carriages! So many cafés! So many theaters! So many places to go! Surely no one starves here; surely everyone must find a job here—it's just a matter of opening one's mouth and saying, "Let it be known that this is what I've decided to do . . . this is how much I'd like to earn."

The women had the whole thing nicely worked out; it was very simple. The mother would enter a house, one that was proper, decent, owned by real gentry, and become a housekeeper, a proper position for a serious and respectable person—anything rather than lose the dignity of one born to a good background, a "distinguished" family of doctors and pharmacists, not farmhands . . .

The older daughter would also serve, but, it must be understood, in a place where she would be treated as befits a well-brought-up young lady, where her honor would be in no danger, and where, eventually, the ladies of the house might look on her as a friend and an equal—who knows? If she found benevolent souls, she might even be considered another daughter. Of course, they would not make her dine with the other servants—she would eat alone, on a very clean table. As for the younger daughter, a ten-year-old, ah! Nothing could be simpler! They would place her in one of those free schools where girls receive a good education and it doesn't cost the parents a dime. Of course! They had planned all this from the moment they set out for the capital.

The women were very surprised when they realized that things were not so easy. Matters became complicated, awfully complicated. At first, two or three of the father's friends had offered to help, to give them references. When reminded of their offer, they responded with delaying tactics, with vague and disturbing words: "It's very difficult . . . the devil take it . . . Such houses can no longer be found . . . Schools are very hard to find . . . There isn't even work for those who don't wish to board . . . Everything is bad . . . Madrid has become impossible."

Those friends—indifferent friends—naturally had their own affairs to attend to, which were much more important to them than the affairs of others. Besides, just try placing three women who are looking for good lodging, decent employers, the moon! Two country women who have never worked. Very honest women, yes—but what good is honesty? Better to be attractive, to know how to get on . . .

One of these friends asked the mother, offhandedly:

"Doesn't the girl know a song or two? Can't she dance? Can't she play the guitar?"

And as the mother was scandalized, he added:

"Don't be shocked, doña María. Sometimes, in the provinces, girls learn these things. Barbers there are teachers—I met one."

A week later, the same friend—a pharmacist, by the way—came to see the two now beleaguered women in their small warren of a rooming house, where they were already sadly late in paying for the wretched bed and the tasteless stew. And after many circumlocutions, he let them know there was a position. Yes, a real job for the girl.

"Don't think it's something to look down on, on the contrary . . . it's very good—lots of tips. Perhaps one duro a day worth of tips, or more. If the girl takes pains with the work, more, I'm sure. But . . . I don't know if you . . . Perhaps you would prefer a different type of job . . . The thing is that the other kind . . . can't be found. In houses they say, 'We want a girl who has experience. We don't want to break in colts.' Whereas here she could be broken in. She can . . ."

"And what position is this?" mother and daughter asked eagerly.

"It's . . . It's just across from my business—at a well-known beer hall. It's work that's hardly work. Women do everything. I could see the girl frequently, because I go to pass the time there in the afternoons. There is music, dancing. It's very nice."

The castaways looked at each other. They understood.

"Thank you, no. My daughter—is not fit for that kind of work," the mother's bourgeois modesty protested.

"No—no, anything else, but not that," the girl declared in turn, blushing.

They parted. It was dusk, a delicious hour. The women's eyes were like swollen fists. Madrid, with its luxury, its radiant spring gaiety, seemed to them a cruel desert, a wilderness where beasts prowled. An encounter with a flower girl brightened for an instant the emaciated face of the young country woman.

"Mama! Roses!" she exclaimed with childish impulsiveness.

"If only we had bread for your little sister!" the mother almost sobbed.

And they were silent. Heads bowed, they retired to their wretched boardinghouse.

A confrontation awaited them. The owner was not exactly a heartless woman: at first she had been patient. She took an interest in the women in mourning, in the little girl, who was sweet and affectionate—who, always waiting for the "free school," didn't consider herself beneath working in the kitchen, helping wash dishes, breaking them, and brushing off the clothes of cash-paying boarders. But everything has its limits, and three mouths are too many to feed, however you feed them. After all, doña Marciala, the owner, was not a Rothschild and could not blindly follow the impulses of her good heart. When she saw the country women return and sit down at the table, expecting the meager stew meat and the noodle soup, she sent the servant to them with a message:

"Doña Marciala asks that you please come to her room."

"What is the matter?"

"I don't know."

The matter was that "things couldn't continue in this way"—that they had to give her something, at least something of what they owed her, or it would be best, "my dears," to clear out. That very day she had had to pay the baker and the grocer. She had had quite a morning! Two brutes—real animals—voices raised, spitting out obscenities in the parlor, threatening to put a lien on the furniture if they didn't get paid, calling her a slippery cheat, her, doña Marciala Galcerán, a lady all her life. "My dears," something had to be done. One who lived from hand to mouth couldn't feed others; it was hard enough to feed oneself. Times were terrible. And she was really very sorry, she regretted it deeply . . . but that was it. She could not extend any more credit to them. That night—well, of course, they would have their dinner—but the next day, either they paid even a little something or they looked for other lodging.

There were tears, laments, a fainting spell from the elder daughter. The castaways saw themselves wandering through the streets, without a roof over their heads, without bread. Their only recourse was to take the last remnants of the past to the pawnshop: the father's gold watch, the mother's trinkets. The money went to doña Marciala . . . and they were still in debt.

"Dears—well—it's better than nothing. I won't bother you for two more weeks. I've paid those Zulus. But think about how you're going to improve your situation, because if you don't . . . What do you *expect*? Madrid has gone sky-high."

And the women began to scurry, to knock on closed doors—which did not open—to read advertisements in the paper, and even to offer themselves to ladies who walked by, asking in an ingratiating and humble tone:

"Would you know of a house where help is needed? Special service, provided by a decent person, who has been in a more fortunate position . . . as a housekeeper, or a chaperone . . ."

The shrugging of shoulders, vague murmurs, a distracted inquiry about specifics, even dry, harsh, scornful rejections . . . The castaways looked at each other. The daughter bowed her head. The same unspoken thought hid in both women. A complicity silently united them. It was obvious that being proper, quite proper, was worth nothing. If her father, may he rest in peace, had been *like others* . . . they would not be in this position, amid the waves, sinking up to their necks . . .

One afternoon they passed in front of the pharmacy. The cheek of that pharmacist! It was unheard-of!

"Why don't we go in?" the mother ventured.

"Let's see . . . if he mentions the job again," the daughter stammered. And with a sorrowful gesture, she added: "A woman can be good anywhere . . ."

FEMINIST

When Pardo Bazán wrote "Feminist," her largely fruitless efforts to incite a feminist conscience in the Spanish public had left her discouraged; it was just four years later that she published her two cookbooks as the final volumes in the Woman's Library. Toward the end of her life, she unreservedly identified herself with the word that forms the title of this story: "I am a radical feminist. I believe that all the rights that men enjoy should also be enjoyed by women" (Carmen Bravo-Villasante, Vida y obra de Emilia Pardo Bazán: Correspondencia amorosa con Pérez Galdós *[Madrid: Magisterio Español, 1973] 292). However, when she compared the state of women's rights with that found in other countries, she pronounced Spain sorely lacking: "Contemporary Spanish women are two centuries younger (or older, depending on one's point of view) than other women in other nations. So there is no feminist movement in Spain in any sense of the word" ("La mujer española,"* Blanco y negro, *5 Jan. 1907: 2).*

When we take into account Pardo Bazán's explicit commentary on feminism, then, this story's title seems ambiguous: does it describe the female protagonist or is Pardo Bazán playing here with the negative conceptions of feminism prevalent during her time? (For that matter, the word feminist *today is just as negative to many.) Is the author poking fun at the emasculating image of feminists, or is she upholding it? Finally, we might ask whose voice is repre-*

118

sented in the title—the author's, the narrator's, or perhaps the male protagonist's?

It was at the Aguasacras spa[1] that I met the couple: the husband, of peevish and tiresome disposition, dragged down by the incurable affliction that two years later took him to the grave; the wife, pretty enough, with her look of happy resignation, solicitously caring for him, always ready to tend to those whims to which the sick are prone and that are their revenge on the healthy.

The valetudinarian nevertheless retained enough energy to discuss all matters human and divine with barely contained irritation and ill-tempered pessimism, discoursing on rigid, uncompromising theories. His manner of thinking was somewhere between inquisitorial and Jacobinic, a more common mixture than one would expect here, where extremes have not only met but often fused into strange amalgams. But the gifts of flexibility and delicacy of spirit, which engender a kind tolerance, are relatively rare among us; and our heated and strident disputes in cafés, gatherings, meetings, plazas, and taverns would demonstrate this, if evidence of a historical nature was lacking.

The invalid to whom I refer could let nothing be. Rare was the person whom he did not judge harshly.

---

[1] "Aguasacras" means "holy water."

The times did not bode well, he said, and the decline of good manners was horrifying. Anarchy reigned in the home because women, without the guiding principle of authority, no longer knew how to be wives, nor did men exercise their prerogatives as husbands and fathers. Modern ideas were corrosive, and the aristocracy, for its part, contributed to the scandal. Until the day came when socks were once again darned, there would be no salvation. The weak character of men explained the impudence and ceaseless chatter of women, who had forgotten that they were born to fulfill a duty, to suckle their children and skim off the soup . . . Noticing that the good man's sermons became all the more animated when he discovered me in his presence, I decided to agree with him so that he would not overexcite himself.

I don't know what struck me most, the intemperance of the husband's constant verbal assaults or the silent and enigmatic little smile of his companion. I have already said that she had a pleasant face, was short and slender, had dark black eyes, and her body displayed the small and steely disposition that promises long life and makes little old ladies as dry and healthy as sugared raisins. Usually her presence—a glance from her—was enough to cut short the husband's diatribes and Catilinarian speeches. It wasn't necessary for her to whisper:

"Don't get all worked up, Nicolás; you know what the doctor said."

Usually the sick man would rise to his feet before reaching this state and, limping, steadied by his better half's arm, would retire or take a short walk among the luxuriant plane trees.

I had completely forgotten the couple—just as one forgets the cinematographic figures, charming or repulsive, that parade by for a fortnight at the spa—when I read the obituary on the fourth page of the newspaper: "The honorable Don Nicolás Abréu y Lallana, Chief of Staff . . . his disconsolate widow, the honorable Doña Clotilde Pedregales . . ." Two days later, chance led me to a meeting on the street with the medical director of Aguasacras, a man keenly observant and very discreet, who had come to Madrid to attend to his professional affairs; and we looked back upon those who had passed away, including the scowling gentleman with the abrasive opinions.

"Ah! Mr. Abréu! The man with the trousers!" the doctor remarked, laughing.

"The man with the trousers?" I asked, curious.

"You don't know about that? I'm surprised, as there are no secrets in spas, and not only had this been discovered, it was commented on with relish. Well! It is true that you left a few days before the Abréus, and people

121

laughed hardest at the end, when they found out . . . You wonder how people get to know what happens behind closed doors. It's amazing. You would almost think there are goblins . . .

"In this particular case, what happened right there at the spa must have been overheard by eavesdropping chambermaids, who are not bad spies, or by the neighbors through the thin walls, or . . . In brief, one of life's strange twists. Apparently the events leading up to what happened were known, because back when he was a newlywed, Abréu, who had to have been the most solemn pain in the neck, went around bragging about it as some sort of clever stunt, as a mark of character, which all men would do well to imitate so as to firmly establish their place as head of the family.

"And, you see, the two episodes complement each other. It's true that Abréu, like all those who become severe moralists at age forty, had had a wild youth full of diversion. He was brought into line by ailments and indispositions and at that point decided to get married, in the same way people decide to move into healthier lodgings. He found a girl, Clotildita, who was pretty, well-bred, and had absolutely no position, and her parents willingly gave her to him, because Abréu, a man of good connections, always had excellent jobs. They were married—and the morning after the wedding, when

the bride awoke, still dazed by the change in her life,
she heard the groom order her, half imperious, half
grinning:

"'Clotilde, dear . . . get up!'

"The young woman did so, without realizing what
was afoot; and immediately the husband commanded,
even more imperiously:

"'Now . . . put on my trousers!'

"Astonished, not believing her ears, the young girl decided to smile herself, thinking that perhaps this was
some sort of honeymoon joke . . . a rather disconcerting
one, rather out of line . . . but, who knows. Might it be
the fashion among newlyweds?

"'Did you hear?' he repeated. 'Put on my trousers!
Right now, my child!'

"Confused, ashamed, and now feeling more like crying than laughing, Clotilde obeyed as best she could.
Obedience is the law!

"'Now sit there,' the husband ordered again, suddenly
solemn and grave, pointing to an armchair. And when
the trouser-clad girl slumped into the armchair, he said,
'I wanted you to wear the trousers at this particular moment so that you would know, my dear Clotilde, that
you will never in your life put them on again. It is I who
will wear them, God willing, every hour and every day,
as long as our marriage lasts, and may it last for many

years in holy peace, amen. Now you know. You may take them off.'

"What did Clotilde think of the warning? She told no one; she kept the absolute, impenetrable silence which so often masks the loss of an ideal, that humble, feminine ideal that is so honorable and so youthful, that asks for love, not servitude . . . She lived submissively and in silence, and if the Roman matron's motto 'She diligently tended the hearth and spun the wool' did not apply to her, it was only because today's textile factories have consigned the spinning wheel and the darning egg to the rubbish heap.

"But in spite of a wholesome marriage, Abréu had buckshot in his wings. The remnants of his ill-spent youth resurfaced unexpectedly in chronic ailments, and the first time he consulted me in Aguasacras, I knew there was no cure; what was palliated could be cured only in the Fountain of Youth . . . If only we knew where it flows!

"His wife cared for him with true self-sacrifice, that we all know. She lived only for him, and instead of seeking amusement for herself—after all, she was still young— she thought of nothing but potions and medicines. But—every morning, when the husband rose from the comfort of his bed—a sweet little voice piped out an order, unequivocal, despite its warbling tone:

"'Put on my petticoat, dear Nicolás! Hurry, put on my petticoat!'

"Without fail, the sick man's face would become contorted; silent curses would rise to his lips . . . the order was always repeated in a chirping voice, and the man would bow his head and clumsily tie around his waist the ribbons from the lace-adorned skirt. And then his gentle wife would add, in a tone no less delicate and musical:

"'Just so you know that now you must wear it for the rest of your life, as long as I am your little nurse. Understand?'

"And Abréu would remain in women's underclothes for quite a while, swearing under his breath, either out of rage or because his rheumatism was acting up, while Clotilde, scurrying about the room, prepared what was needed for the numerous painful treatments, the therapeutic massages, and the prescribed flannel wrappings."

THE CIGARETTE STUB

"The Cigarette Stub" seems to begin where "Torn Lace" leaves off. The male protagonist proceeds with the idea that responses to trivial incidents can reveal character. Searching for a suitable spouse—that is, one who will be ever docile and even-tempered—he decides to submit each candidate to a test. He purposely provokes each potential wife; the one who maintains her sweet composure is the winner. But the test backfires; the protagonist has not judged feminine—or human—nature as accurately as he had thought.

The narrative dynamics of the story are subtle. While the perspective of the man is presented virtually throughout, the narrator maintains a distance from him, at several points inserting commentary that ironically undermines the protagonist's thoughts and actions. In their strikingly different images and in the different ways the protagonists approach the "significant insignificant," this story and "Torn Lace" form an intriguing pair.

Having resolved to get married—marriage being one of those things nobody fails to do, sooner or later—Cristóbal Morón set out to probe the character of a few young ladies among those he most fancied, ladies whom he judged to have the traits he considered necessary for the establishment of a happy household.

126

First and foremost, it was Cristóbal's wish that the woman he would one day lead to the proverbial altar be of excellent disposition, even-tempered, tranquil, and rather jovial, quite above being provoked to irritation and anger by trivial incidents. Outbursts of anger might be short-lived but, when recurrent, were certain to sour conjugal life. An ever-smiling countenance and never-ending agreeableness—that was Cristóbal's feminine ideal.

He was not unaware of the degree to which marriageable women, generally speaking, hid their true personalities. For that reason, he wanted to surprise the woman he chose with one of those innocent ruses that sometimes reveal people's characters in spite of themselves. And he devised something ingenious but very simple and absolutely foolproof.

When he set his sights on a young woman, Cristóbal would begin by addressing her in a way that, instead of being amorous in the true sense of the word, was charming and easygoing. When he saw her at nighttime socials or during the day at outdoor gatherings, he would sit down next to her, chat gaily and sweetly, banter with her, ask her about her tastes and ideas—sometimes teasing her playfully, sometimes affecting sympathy and agreement with her opinions—all the while trying to plumb the depths of her spirit. After taking her measure for a while, he would unexpectedly commit one of those involuntary acts of clumsiness unique to men: he would tramp on her dress, bump into her plumed coiffure, wrecking it completely—in short, do something that could provoke an immediate outburst of anger through which the true nature of the woman would show itself. And such outbursts always occurred—with suddenness and violence.

"My God!" Cristóbal would exclaim to himself. "What a hornet's nest I was about to get into."

Abandoning one woman in port, he would set sail with another, resolved not to enter serious relations until he had determined where the important boundaries lay.

Eventually, it was in Sarito Vilomara that Cristóbal felt he had at last found what he sought: the yearned-for angel who would take a bachelor's heart under her protective wings—a heart that had become bored with venal, stormy romances, with inns where invariably he ate the same French omelet and kidneys in sherry at the same hour and in the company of the same friends who borrowed and forgot to repay.

Sarito (a diminutive for the very Spanish name Rosario) was a gay and vivacious young woman, docile as a dove (though actually doves have little about them that is docile), who of course presented herself to Cristóbal in a self-effacing manner that suited completely his every idea and theory, always complying with whatever he proposed.

A light touch of roguish contrariness—immediately dissolving into submissiveness—rendered her excessive malleability and complaisance less bland. Helped along by eyes that demanded "surrender," dark silky tresses around a dimpled face, and a fresh and blossomlike mouth, Cristóbal began to see in Sarito the woman of his dreams. Nonetheless, he did not want to rely on that impression without having put the woman's sweet and equable temperament to the test.

He took advantage of an especially propitious occasion for the test. One evening, as they departed from a soirée under a heavy downpour, Sarito, who was in the company of her mother, offered Cristóbal a ride in the spare seat of their carriage. They were barely under way when her father casually lit a cigarette and offered one to the man who he already considered to be his future son-in-law.

"Been a long time since I last smoked!" he exclaimed. "Imagine not having a smoking room in that house . . ."

Permission having been granted, Cristóbal accepted and lighted the cigarette, as Sarito sweetly held the match for him. This was a moment when the suitor felt he was madly in love. He cast a deep, consuming look at the woman, and she responded with her own, full of relish and curiosity about this new sensation. She was gorgeous, divinely attired. Her white crepe overcoat was

129

exquisite with its silver embroidery and tassels. Despite all this, Cristóbal did not forget. On the contrary. The realization that he was caught in Cupid's snare gave him such a fright that he found himself employing his customary trick. As if by accident, he dropped the burning cigarette onto the delicate fabric of the coat. It quickly caught fire. Cristóbal waited for the usual impatient outburst. But nothing of the sort occurred. With a most natural aplomb, with laughter like pearl beads slipping from their string, Sarito brushed off the ash, pinched out the spreading point of fire between her lovely fingers, and exclaimed:

"It's no problem . . . It's nothing . . . Don't worry about it . . ."

Cristóbal saw heaven open above him. This was *the* divine woman, the one who rose above minor inconveniences, not letting them change the beautiful equilibrium of her sweet disposition. The following day, he proposed. Six months later, they were married.

Cristóbal saved in a glass case the stub of the cigarette he had used for the test. He embarked on the customary honeymoon journey with his wife, and the golden veil of well-deserved happiness prevented him from seeing the gradual change in Sarito's style and character. The enthusiasm for life that seemed so characteristic of her turned into an unrelenting insistence on the satisfaction of her every whim, even the most extravagant. Nothing satisfied the bride, and nothing the groom chose escaped small but wounding objections that pricked like thorns. Moments of bliss were always followed by trivial quarrels that often degenerated into arguments and rancorous complaints. Cristóbal viewed all this in the best light: he was still intoxicated, and he attributed his wife's change of mood to the fact that the trip had taken them out of their routine. He resolutely believed that when they had settled into a tranquil domestic life, under the calming influence of the lares and penates, Sarito would once again be the charming young woman of happy mien and peaceable character who had bewitched him so.

After taking up residence in the *hôtel* where they lodged their happiness, Cristóbal soon noticed, to his horror, that his wife continued to be as she had been during the honeymoon. It could even be said that the acrimony had increased and become the norm. At his wit's end, Cristóbal searched for the source of this most peculiar transformation. He tried everything to please his companion. Lavish gifts, gallantries, every sort of elegant courtesy had no effect. Sarito had forgotten the laughter that put dimples in her cheeks, the benign acceptance that made her face radiate a joyful beauty. Cristóbal was now afraid of approaching his wife, and putting his arm around her waist in an affectionate caress seemed most problematic.

As he was submerged in a feeling of misfortune, a sort of superstitious faith awoke in him: he thought of his fetish, the cigarette stub that had decided his fate. Out at the theater one evening with his wife, he respectfully, devotedly, lit up that same stub. Sarito wore an elegant boa of ruffled tulle interwoven with gossamer feathers. He removed the cigarette from his lips and pressed it to the diaphanous garment until it began to burn. Sarito turned on him like a viper.

"You ass! Watch what you're doing!"

Cristóbal dropped his arms without scolding his temperamental wife for her inconsistency.

In the glow of his cigarette and the light smoke from the tulle—quickly extinguished—he began to see clearly the marital error he had made. Sarito's soured spirit, her metamorphosis, had an explanation or, if you will, a motive; and this motive or explanation was the most cruel, the most bitter, and without remedy . . . A woman is sweet and affectionate when she loves; but his wife, if she at one time thought she loved him, had decided, as a result of some critical experience, that she no longer loved him. The flame, which devours what it touches, had gone out like the cigarette instead of blazing brightly during their first attempts at life together. And for that there was no remedy. It was hopeless, like so many things in this world.

He did not protest, he made not the slightest gesture of anger. He resigned himself to the future, with its constant struggles, rather than to toss the rope after the bucket or his honor after his happiness.

Quietly, he entered the theater at his wife's side, where an absurd, comical vaudeville act was being performed.

THE PINK TREE

"The Pink Tree" is Pardo Bazán's last published story. It appeared in Raza española, *in a special memorial number issued shortly after her death. As in "Castaways," a lyrical evocation of the beauty of Madrid is undercut by the mordant twists of the plot. The story is also reminiscent of "My Suicide," in that the protagonist comes to realize that what she perceived as an idyllic romance was in fact nothing of the kind. But her response to her disillusionment is markedly different from that of the protagonist of the earlier story. The surprise ending of "My Suicide" also presents an interesting contrast to the quiet, oblique way in which Pardo Bazán ends her final story.*

For the couple, who met secretly in Retiro Park,[1] the pink tree served as a point of rendezvous: "You know, under the tree . . ."

They could have met anywhere else instead of at that arboreal bouquet, whose vivid color stood out against the green backdrop of the rest of the trees. It was just

---

[1] The Retiro is a huge wooded public park in the middle of Madrid, occupying over three hundred acres and complete with flower beds, a lake, statues, and even a crystal palace. Originally the Retiro formed the grounds of a palace built by Felipe IV in the seventeenth century. It has been open to the public since the eighteenth century.

134

that the pink tree had a youthful charm and seemed to them the emblem of their love, a love that had been born on the streets and that dominated them more forcefully every day.

He was a lad of twenty-five who, according to his own account, had come to Madrid on business. Two days after his arrival, while he stood in front of a jeweler's storefront display, he exchanged the first meaningful glance with Milagros Alcocer. She had just attended mass at San José and was taking her morning stroll, browsing in stores and hearing the trifling nonsense at her back that any young woman who is not bad-looking hears when she roams about the streets. The man decided to follow Milagros that morning, keeping a few steps behind and stopping on the sidewalk when he saw her stop in front of a window. He said nothing to her. Silent, absorbed in his thoughts, he gazed at her ardently, projecting a kind of magnetism through his dark eyes with their long lashes. And when she set out for home, he followed her as if he were doing the most natural thing in the world. He even caught up to her, whispering:

"Don't be frightened. I don't want to disturb you. Why don't you stop for a moment, so we can talk?"

She quickened her pace, and that was that for the day. The moment Milagros set foot in the street the next day, she saw her pursuer, all smiles and dressed more neatly and more carefully than the day before. He approached her brazenly and walked alongside her as if sure of her acquiescence. Milagros felt a confused numbing of her will; nonetheless, she recovered some degree of equanimity and whispered quietly and with anguish:

"Please don't walk next to me. My father, my brother, or a girlfriend might see us. There could be a scene! I don't even want to think about it!"

"Well, where should I wait for you? Tell me. Where?"

She hesitated. She was about to answer, "Nowhere." Her heart was racing. Finally she made up her mind, and murmured quietly, filled with anxiety:

"At the Retiro. There is a pink tree to the left. The whole tree is like a bouquet . . . there in the park."

And she started off, almost at a run, toward Alcalá Street. He held back discreetly and finally followed in the same direction. He didn't see her when he reached the tree. But she appeared in a moment. She arose from a nearby bench, all flushed with emotion. In a matter of moments they understood each other, rushing headlong into happiness. He had fallen in love with her at first sight. She, for her part, didn't know what had happened; but she understood now that more or less the same thing had happened to her as well. How strange! She had never dreamed of a sweetheart, never held anybody in her heart. Her father was a clerk; her mother had died. She enjoyed quite a bit of freedom but never used this liberty for any kind of mischief. This was the first time she would have to hide something at home. Full of passion, he soothed her emotions. Now, was she doing anything wrong? She was following the impulses of her heart, and that is the most natural thing in the world. Men and women are attracted to each other by an inescapable law, and that is the most beautiful thing in life. What a sorry state we'd be in if love didn't exist! What would this park be like without its pink tree!

He spoke energetically and persuasively, and in a lyrical manner, like someone who knows life or is trying to control it, and he squeezed Milagros's hands in his own, transmitting his warmth and desire to her. The young woman felt all the sensations of one who is slipping down a wet slope toward a deep well. Her reason, almost obliterated, nonetheless gave off a spark of light. Who was this fellow who had captivated her so? Where did he come from, what did he do? Was he, at the very least, a good man, an honest man? When they found a bench in a solitary corner, Milagros overwhelmed her companion with questions, without thinking how easy it was for a person to say one thing while meaning something quite different. But he answered her questions in a tone that seemed quite sincere. He confided his past to her; his name was Raimundo Corts; at first a common working man, through force of will and ability he had become the manager of a textile factory in Lérida. Lots of work, a comfortable income! "But," he warned with polite *you*, since they had not yet begun to use the familiar forms of speaking, "if I wanted to buy you one of those jewels you were looking at yesterday in the store window, I couldn't. Though there are people who without having to work can give jewels like that, or better ones still. Unfair, *no l'sembla?*"[2]

She certainly was in no frame of mind to get lost in sociological treatises. They spoke of their affection and agreed to meet every day, without fail, at the pink tree. He suggested places that were less poetic and more hidden, but Milagros surprised herself in her capacity to resist that impulse. "No," she repeated. "Not that. Here it seems to me I'm doing nothing wrong. Somewhere else . . . no. Don't ask that of me." The young man's eyes blazed with passion; to those who could read the language of the soul through a man's eyes, he was saying, "You will give in, you have no choice; you love me too much to refuse much longer." At the same time she too was calculating in her mind; because love also calculates, as if it were a merchant or a moneylender: "How is a love such as mine to end, if not in marriage? We will marry,

---

[2] Catalan for "don't you think so?"

we'll go to Lérida, we'll live happily ever after. But we need to let some time pass . . . and try to keep this carriage on track. If I rush into this, he will lose his respect for me." Her bourgeois honor protected her, and both the attack and the defense continued under the embracing shade of the pink tree, every last blossom aflame under the illuminating caress of the springtime sun.

One day, to her surprise—the most common things surprise us, as if we weren't expecting them—Milagros noticed that the pink tree was losing its color. Its small flowers fell from the branches and began to carpet the ground. This simple event weighed down her heart, as if it were a great misfortune. Instinctively, she felt that the fate of her love was linked to that of the tree. As if to confirm this superstitious apprehension, that very day Raimundo arrived gloomy and sullen, like someone who has something sad to say but is reluctant to confess it. Instead of explaining the cause of his dejection, he insisted on repeating the same old nagging question: Weren't they ever going to meet in a safer and freer place? Wasn't it absurd that they knew no shelter other than this tree, as if Madrid weren't a large city and one couldn't live comfortably in it? He complained that she didn't love him, that she said no because she was a plaster statue.

The young woman then seemed to regain her courage, to make up her mind. She had said no, she replied, because she had thought there was something more between them, something worthy, something serious. Didn't he think so too? Or had he only wanted distraction, to amuse himself for a few days while he was on his trip?

He bowed his head and scowled; his face hardened, and a sharp furrow cut across his youthful, smooth forehead. Finally he blurted out a few embarrassing words. Yes, no doubt . . . What she said was quite true . . . except that this wasn't the right time to be thinking about such things. Such things had to be thought out carefully to avoid any rash decisions. He had matters of great importance pending, serious matters that he couldn't abandon from one day to the next, and he himself did not know how far they'd take him. Who knew whether he'd have to emigrate, to leave for foreign lands? He wasn't one of those men who never changed jobs. His busy life could be the subject of a novel . . . That's why they should enjoy this moment of happiness, why they should get together where no one could limit the bounds of their joy. . .

"No?" he asked.

"No! No that. Never, love of my life!"

Crestfallen, pale, he didn't reply. He took a tiny branch from the pink tree and put it in his vest pocket. When they said good-bye, they agreed to meet next day. "At the same time, right?"

That night Milagros received a succinct letter by courier. Raimundo had to leave; he had been informed by telegram that his presence was urgently needed. He would write soon.

But he never did. The young woman waited in vain for another letter. She cried a lot, she had sick headaches and nervous upsets; yet she had the impression she had avoided some great danger. What danger? She couldn't define it. Didn't that man love her? Why did he pretend so? Who was he? With great skill and with the assistance of a girlfriend, she managed to investigate matters in Lérida, and it turned out that Raimundo Corts was unknown there.

She grew weary of feeling regret, of pining and watching the days go by and waiting for him to appear under the pink tree, whose blossoms had fallen to the ground. She began to console herself, and sometimes she thought she had dreamed the whole romance.

Some time later she married an uncle of hers who came back from Cuba "with money." Strolling through the Retiro one spring day holding a small child by the hand, she looked toward the pink tree. It was again ablaze, all atremble in flowers. It was gently swaying in the breeze.